BARRY STARK'S
WARM LEATHER

BARRY STARK'S
WARM LEATHER

FRANK VERDUZCO LOPEZ

Gotham Books
30 N Gould St.
Ste. 20820, Sheridan, WY 82801
https://gothambooksinc.com/

Phone: 1 (307) 464-7800

© 2022 Frank V. Lopez. All rights reserved.

No part of this book may be reproduced, stored in a retrieval system, or transmitted by any means without the written permission of the author.

Published by Gotham Books (October 7, 2022)

ISBN: 979-8-88775-091-0 (sc)
ISBN: 979-8-88775-092-7 (e)

Because of the dynamic nature of the Internet, any web addresses or links contained in this book may have changed since publication and may no longer be valid.

The views expressed in this work are solely those of the author and do not necessarily reflect the views of the publisher, and the publisher hereby disclaims any responsibility for them.

PURE MAINSTREAM FICTION

"A NEW YORK METRO DRAMA"

IT IS OFTEN SAID LOVE COMES AND GOES, BUT EVEN THE DEADLIEST, NOT NECESSARILY SO QUIETLY. IT WAS NO MIRCACLE. THE NIGHT'S JACKAL, A MOTORCYCLE COP, IN HIS LAWLESSNESS, DECIDED THAT HE WOULD BE THE MASTE AND WOULD SERVE JUSTICE IN FRONT OF THE LADY, WITH THE BLIND-FOLD AND THE SCALE.

Contents

INTRODUCTION: 9

CHAPTER 1: THE SCENT OF A PSYCHOTIC COP 11
CHAPTER 2: THE MIDST'S OF FASHION 17
CHAPTER 3: SCREAMING HEADLINES 29
CHAPTER 4: THE APARTMENT 32
CHAPTER 5: UNSYMPATHETIC AND CRUEL 36
CHAPTER 6: STANDING ORDERS 38
CHAPTER 7: DUTY ON THE PROWL 40
CHAPTER 8: THE SCARLET DRESS 48
CHAPTER 9: GUILT AND DECEPTION 51
CHAPTER 10: THE DOMESTIC SITUATION 58
CHAPTER 11: STYMIED AND ON THE CARPET 61
CHAPTER 12: THE INSANITY COMES 67
CHAPTER 13: CLOUDLESS AND COLD 74
CHAPTER 14: FLOWERS FOR MY LADY 79
CHAPTER 15: TRAPPED AND CORNERED 82
CHAPTER 16: THE COVER GIRL 87
CHAPTER 17: THE ACQUISITION 93
CHAPTER 18: WINDOW OF HOPE 104
CHAPTER 19: PATROLLING THE BOULEVARD 113
CHAPTER 20: THE POWER OF LOVE 117
CHAPTER 21: THE HEAT IS ON 126

CHAPTER 22: RELIEVED FROM DUTY 132
CHAPTER 23: ON THE RUN 138
CHAPTER 24: THE KNOCK ON THE DOOR 143
CHAPTER 25: HIDING IN PLAIN SIGHT 150
CHAPTER 26: SAINT PATRICK'S DAY 155
CHAPTER 27: MAGICAL THINKING... 157
CHAPTER 28: THE PROTESTERS 161
CHAPTER 29: CLOSED-CASKET 183
CHAPTER 30: PRELUDE TO WARM LEATHER 185

INTRODUCTION:
A BLOODY SIN

He was a psychopath that lures his bright greenish eyes on victims. With a promise they can't resist and demands a payment no person could willingly think to pay. The young and vulnerable, the attractive models made the perfect target, the street walkers made the best prey. The recruits were many but naïve an extremely susceptible as they appeared. These young ladies had a lot to learn about New York City. One night this lonely model made irresistible bait for the charismatic motorcycle cop. That could not be trusted with her life-but could not guarantee to be strong enough to refrain from this man in spite of the temptation. He was like a hunter, hunting human flesh a most terrifying face to face terminator. Shaking even the lone-lily, soulless not powerful or strong enough to battle this psycho, who is less than a human being. If the nature of this beast is right you will be saddened by the rise and fall of this man in uniform. In the city where big money was as easy to make, and just as easy to spend-away where if you kick it into over drive a good job can get anything you want, and what it will cost you in the very end optically or financial. In this story of two broken people, who clashed together, and were forever interwoven. With his own sense of reality, Barry Stark had a pretty good life up to now with a loving family and job when a situation takes a drastic turn into a dark spinning world and its fringes. Yes, this is the story of one man on the metro police force and how he fell off on the road to Payton place. Barry was drawn to an It Girl and her ambition and desire to get the best of good intensions. His deceptive efforts to keep pace with her would wreak all kinds of havoc in his sense of self. The bar was set high with disastrous results but the times were exquisitely suspenseful both emotionally heart wrenching and thoroughly satisfying. As remote as it sounds there were no solitary lives to be found in this big city. In the opening pages something horrible should be happening but what could keep one guessing?

Some literary critics may write; The story of Barry Stark's Warm Leather doesn't work too hard to make you love or hate him. In the end you will come around with a change of heart to his manly charms and charisma. This is a heartfelt romantic but tragic drama that carries for him a real life-or-death consequence - not just well intention punch lines. But a culture clash of despicable justice in our society like a litmus-test, Barry's character steels one's sympathy. In all fairness it was his insane warp righteousness for justice who took license to kill.......... in other words, it was the insanity that manifested as violations of societal norms and his PTSD state of mind.

THE SCENT OF A PSYCHOTIC COP
CHAPTER 1

IN TRUE HOLLYWOOD tradition, and high adventure, romantic tragedy, and a mix of evil suspense, smack in the center was the worst Police precinct in the entire nation, New York City's Metro P. D. Where young rookie cops no sooner would flip their badges, against their captain's chest than capitulate to rules, regulations and bureaucratic red tape. GQ cops with thunderous egos, rogues, profane mavericks whose cold stone hearts steep the city's streets in cavalier style. This requiem is not about a cop who chases thugs across the hoods of moving vehicles but about one cynical thirty-one-year-old donning the navy-blue uniform and his own twisted brand of justice. Looking up one could see, set among the stars, the tallest fortress glass buildings of the neon city that stretched upward against the horizon. On one dark street, outside a dilapidated bar of bikers and cronies, a man wielded a Sharpe malevolent-looking switch blade. He created a visually compelling effect. He was a cop like all cops' shunned and abused by society's ills of today, that took advantage of men like him and treated them like a low breed of insect. While this underdog, like a wrecking ball, demonstrated his strength by smashing in his victim's luxuriant black Cadillac with a sledge hammer. As the life slowly pumped out of the man, and was left for dead in a pool of his own blood. His belly had been slit wide open, with the knife blade still wedged deep against his sternum. There was no time of night less dangerous than another. As the ominously black shadow wheeled his motorcycle down the misty alley, suggesting only the supernatural in an undercurrent of terror, the residue of noise left the impacted with overt horror. In the far distance, frantic sires filled the air over the city that festered in night filth. The smell was the natural condition of things. With the closing whine of the last siren, a squad car flipped off its overhead red and blue strobe light. Two tall uniformed cops stepped out, properly geared for action. In the midst of a homicide squad of gold badges, nothing could restrain the course of things now. It had become a police atmosphere, a world blurred, partially erased as feminine and masculine forms stood on cell-phone video watch from the street corner across the way.

"Take the stiff away!" Lieutenant Bloodworth shouted, stumping on his cigarette butt.

After the photographs, the body was taken away. All that remained was a white chalked outline.

"For a pimp, it's too nasty of a kill." The Lieutenant grunted.

"Looks like a revenge kill," Police Chief remarked impressively. Who's the hard-luck character?" Frank March, a reporter for the New York Times asked.

"Kiddo, get out of my hair!" Chief Abraham said, by way of pulling rank.

"This is a case for a veteran reporter," Frank Marsh replied.

"Are you too important to watch where you're going, Marsh?" Chief Abraham sniped as he resumed his movement toward the swelling crowd. Brushing in eager pursuit was Marsh.

Suddenly, Chief Abraham turned around with the suggestion of harbored resentment. "Look! You're like a sword hanging over my head. I've done everything I could to avoid you."

"Say, Abraham! I'm no left-wing sympathizer. I just want a good story for my readers, "Marsh shouted. "A gutsy police track down."
"Marsh, you're disgrace to good journalism. Just what kind of example are you setting for the young fledgling reporters? I hope I've impressed upon your mealy mind how serious this new wave of violence has become," Chief Abraham scolded.

"You're an old fossil! A relic from the past," Marsh intoned as he walked off.

"He is right! This ego maniacal cop must be stopped," Lieutenant Bloodworth insisted in a masterful way. "His rational is surreal madness."

"Yes, and this won't help us with the new recruits," Chief Abraham said as he bit off the end of a cigar and spit it to the asphalt.

"He acts with God-like freedom and high power. This psychopathic cop is on the police force and I want him, "Bloodworth said as the powerful imagery burned in his mind a half hour after the kill.

"Off the record, this lawless knight has behaved with some intelligence. He got Willy-sweet black Willy the pimp. He is officially off our streets."

"It's one way of getting these school-girl prostitutes off the street corners. They're just a mincing chorus of cupids in an age of warped morality."

"Still---this cop will be the toughest case for a criminal defense attorney to try---- because of the innate prejudice built up against one of our own."

"Well, he'll be entitled to the best representation he can get." "Even you can't censor a sick mind."

"There is no more hero worshiping,"The chief said in one brief shining moment.

"Everybody's angry; they don't need any deeper motivation then that!" The chief's voice shook against the curling warm breeze.

"But Chief, you don't always get what we pay for in life." He had dispensed the narrative pleasantries, relying on the chemistry between them.

The news's press there was oddly compelling for an unlikable core of journalist. That had inserted them into the story - they created an interesting diversion in a pathetic way, trying to be most important in this turn of events. The Chief knows every member there and everyone knew him well. Never-the-less he was not glad to see them there like piranhas waiting for a bite of his flesh. But heaven helps those who help themselves or was its God? Was this expression, vainglory for their actions and behavior?

"What a mess they all are?" Captain Tanner inserted himself to the Chief.

"There is no elegance in this violence or hot wit for me. The past few weeks have been pure hell for me." The Chief replayed.

'I thank God for my men, like Barry Stark. He has an impressive string of arrests and willingness to do whatever else that is required of him," Captain Tanner retold.

"He's caught the attention of the department like some shining white knight in our sea of blue uniforms." Chief reiterated. "I'd say worthy of promotion."

"It's not a set of beliefs held by me at this moment and that is the unquestionable truth."

"Same as gospel?"

"There are people in the department that may differ from your opinion regarding the worth of officer Stark. "The chief said to keep him off-balance and walked away".

There were 76 geographical area precincts to keep the mayor's office busy and alert but whom was more warmhearted to the illegals that made the city look more like the Star Wars cantina in midtown New York. The next Day across the street sat Barry Stark and Brent Barrett watching for crazy things to happen on this rough day. Both officers were not on a flossy posse just sitting tight nestled behind a street blockade and waiting. Their raunchy humor ran deep and funny that loosened their threatening posture but predictable sickening thud.

Barry Stark ratcheted up the tension, his misery curdled into a kind of evil that merited crude pervasive language, "You know lieutenant Bloodworth! All he wants is to bust my candy ass. The man can almost taste it, he won't stop until my anus is on a stick and fried like bacon."

"Your right about that bastard! He is anal," Brent said to his hot-tempered partner, "But the Chief has our backs and safety for now."

"You're boring me to tears maybe I should lean over the commode. I'd like to Taser the old fart's sweaty fat butt."

"Well, buddy! You won't see my rosy tushie bending over any time soon to you." In the camaraderie Brent tried to inspire him and create a sense of warmth.

"Still, I hate Bloodworth. I'd cage fight that tootsie boy and finish him off with my baton." Barry shouted mean spirited and spin off on his Harley Davidson over the frustration.

This city was always an epic undertaking for all the men who wore the badge. Then just sending corpses to the morgue or arresting the homeless for public urination and the hookups with escorts in fleabag hotel rooms. Yes, New York was trippy and tantalizing to all visitors who came there to stay or play.

In a heady narrative with a weary smile on his smug face in a matter of a few hours a wild ride on a summer morning Barry Stark had missed his annual physical exam with Doctor Luna. Things were never as bad as they seemed. A good walk would do him good from the hot weather and the sticky sweat on his underwear. Trying to cope emotionally as the local news reporters stirred up trouble as his life became more complicated. When their puzzling news cast reports hit the police, department demanding even more resources for the law enforcement agencies and the Feds to hunt down the precinct's most determined killer cop on the police force. Now making his every step more painful than the last. Barry Stark was now forced to confront his own terrifying events inside his head. If he was to find meaning in his life.

By mid-day the sound of bullets echoed away in a nearby alley. Even in the more impressive silence, a distant church bell rang in the frail impatient dangerous doubt of time. On the worn-down pavement a sports car roared up the street zero to sixty in all of six seconds - did God pour down his wrath on this big city? Maybe the miff solitude was enough shelter from the changing heat wave. Police dressed up in riot black gear confronting protesters, as Barry Stark rode through the seething street. The local and uncompromising misfits welcome him by throwing water bottles filled with bright yellow urine from the flat roof top tenements above. But today he paid them no mind. Breaking through the rush hour traffic like an icebreaker or some battleship behind enemy lines as the sunshine shone through the tallest glass buildings. While the strands of his dark brown hair gleamed in the motorcycle's side mirrors, that did nothing to the darkness in his green shadowed eyes as he placed his helmet back on. Seemingly he had not slept well one might have guessed stopping for a hot-dog lunch. With plenty of muster, onions and pickle relish despite the despair of others who hated cops on this block. Barry was seen as the most powerful man in blue as voices wavered around him for a moment. But he gazed back steadily at them. He knew their thoughts and nodded with a maturity knowing the good men like him did for all of society.

As two skinheads stood on the street corner next to a tattoo parlor. When one of them tossed a lit cigarette onto the pavement. It was no Marlboro as Barry dropped his half eaten lunch into an orange trash bin.

"Look brother! I'm deadly serious and thinking about arresting you for littering!" Barry smelled marijuana.

"Oh! You aren't shitting me cop?" The dirty smelly punk answered.

"Hold it right there! Man you are high and flying on cannabis."

"You're not setting my ass up, cop?" The punk cried in a worn out trench coat.

"No! Your busted!"

"Guilty as charged officer!" The punk took a swing at Barry, he calmly ducked under the swing. The whole skirmish was over in less than ten seconds.

Barry drop kicked the two hundred and fifty-pound doper without breaking a sweat. "I hate you subculture brawlers when you mess my hair up."

"You have the wrong attitude pig!"

"Look! I'm a good judge of bad character, scam bag."

"Judge, jury and executioner."

"You slit your own throat skinhead, when you drop that joint on the ground." Barry said in the safest reply of words in the man's predicament. Even though Barry had a deadly side it was hard to keep the unholy down at times.

THE MIDST'S OF FASHION
CHAPTER 2

A FEW BLOCKS away on another evening of a hot day, caught in heavy traffic a policeman on a gleaming motorcycle answered a 2-11 burglary in progress. The police call came at a red light stop, while loud, crazy rock music filtered out onto the famed Boulevard, from the theaters, bars and nightclubs that lined the sidewalks. In the city without pity, like a hi-tech machine racing along, the wind battered the officer's black and white helmet. His vision became blurred but he was a motorcycle cop who loved the speed the noise and the smell of the gasoline exhaust as he set out to do his duty. A worthy opponent in dark glasses, Barry Stark championing the law that could easily bring him to the brink of prosecution but he had his own agenda chasing dirty thugs in a tangle web and was prepared to kill to protect himself. He was as a man uniquely of this moment adrenalin charged he puffed and wheezed as he protected the very vulnerable with justices served.

There was much going on in the city as the columnist, Mars, a stellar reporter for the local Star newspaper stated, "This looks sinister." Quite candidly, it was not the edifying story he wanted to write. But a modern masterpiece that expanded the horizon of the unpopular media with the police that swept the nation. With the force of a hurricane in this feverish excitement of a cop's murders. Something to grab his readers with eyes wide open over the worst and most riveting cop ever seen on the front pages.

Acting stern and righteous Barry Stark found himself in plenty of unexpected and very risky situations and hated criminals with plenty of money. To pull strings and fat envelopes full of cash to bribe public officials and bad judges in their favor. On this night stopping at nothing, guided by his own experience a cynical wit, ninety percent of the time he behaved like most cops. He had had a spunky instinct for survival in the murk of New York city, a potent combination of past hurts that increased his mood swings.

High volume music filled the grand dining room of the Hyatt Regency Hotel. It had been turned into a fashion showroom, with guests by invitation only, for the socially elite, compliments of Bloomingdales. Suddenly, the scrappy voice of the fashion. commentator, Elaine Gondi, drew the audience's attention. Silhouetted in basic black and wearing thick, large framed glasses, she celebrated in verse. "The boys won't be walking down the street kicking cans this summer. All this according to our young designer, Jerome Lawrence, listen up ladies, you too gents. They won't be looking up at the electric billboards as you walk by on the avenues, being oh so bad and checking out the latest scene as you trip the fantastic. Yes, men will be but fools, summing us up, down and all around this town. They'll whistle from the highest steel girders as you shine in the sunlight, all so fine. Just feast your eyes. Today's female can dress for party-going and to work for the boss. Put the mood on, ladies. Don't be afraid. The colors are right with shots of gold and silver. The fabric is luxurious silk from the silkworm. Who butter flies in the end. So, look out, Country Gals, here come Bloomingdale's big city girls with their patent leather purses, heels and wide belts. Yes, dark and light, opaque stockings with the 1940's seams are the in thing again. Tally-ho! To the night spot of your choice as you go clubbing! What a way to show off the flesh. Turn, turn Summer Harriett!

Swivel those curious hips, Ronnie Love. Aren't these models beautiful? Come on, Dionne Norris, sway, and sway for the spectators, you too, JeZe Bella Reyes. You've just seen our working girls' collection-----enough to ding the old renaissance bell." These were permissive times the night had endurance and would test the body and mind as the lives of

JeZe Bella Reyes and Barry Stark are forever altered through a chance meeting. This is how their story unfolded enticingly with summer in full swing, under a spot light a Model holding an umbrella in a black cat suit. It was the Fashion's Summer Preview and all the top Designers want-to-be' there to be seen among the celebrity of stars. Outside sirens could be heard. As this cop pulls over to curbside, smiling ferociously with perfect white teeth and tan face, licking his dry lips he explodes into laughter like a response to the sort of humor that veers from a men's football locker room. Straddling off the motorcycle he dropped his gold pen to the gutter. With his butt shimmying left to right he bent to pick it up as the gun on his hips swayed. There was no doubt about his profession, inbred and refine, he even walked like a Bengal Tiger on the hunt, feared and proud.

Behind the scenes of the mock-up designer showroom, Officer Barry Stark emerges from the exit backstage. He is observed as a hard hitting, tough talking realist in a gossamer world of fantasy and high fashion. He is every inch the tall, lean and ruggedly handsome motorcycle cop in his *warm leather* jacket, shiny black boots and gleaming white helmet. Like the ancient stargazers were guided by a fleeting moment, sensual, and natural investigating the circumstance of a minor crime. JeZe Bella's dark eyes followed the police officer's manly finger as he pointed to her. Squeezing through the backstage crew in a style that made a splash, she was a slender 5'8" model who dreamed of fame and real fortune. Taking her aside officer Stark created electricity with his body movement, searching her out amiably his green eyes were warmly admiring. At first glance, several questions sprang to his mind. While he entered into a small computerized notebook her name, and pertinent information, looking like a unique challenge, Barry Stark lingers to provoke the sensual curiosity of the long raven-hair model. JeZe Bella Reyes, who's now intrigued by his certain conflicting qualities and behavior that would be considered of a controlling nature as he was drawn to her glamorous aura, a strange impulse came over him. As the other models' natural tendencies regarded and observed them both by motivation or other reasons. Although Stark was well aware of their measuring and glowing glances under the heat of the sizzle of lights above them, he did not look away from the Latin beauty before him. Almost self-consciously he was certain she viewed him with a kind of distrust as he regarded her expressionlessly and said, "This is a striking turnabout! I came out here on a burglary in process and found it to be another nasty mugging."

"Well, it all happened-so-fast officer!"

"You don't have to be afraid of me. I'm an officer of the law whose only motive is to help you. Please my name is Barry Stark." With little effort, he winked and smiled boyishly as he pushed a finger up against his gold badge and number.

By now, JeZe Bella had managed to compose herself, running her well-manicured fingers through her long, jet black hair almost self-consciously. She managed a smile, "Yes, I was knocked down by a teenaged assailant. He took my cash and dropped my purse, then ran from the dressing room up the hall and out the back exit. One of the security guards chased the kid across the parking garage but lost him."

Stark grinned supportively, "That sounds pretty brutal?" he emotionally patted her on the shoulder, "Tell you what, if you're real good and stop worrying, I'll take you dancing my first night off. That's a promise!" by this time, he had established enough of a rapport to tease her.

Amid the wagging tongues of her nearby associates, she noticed more than he did. "You've raised a few eyebrows, Officer Stark."

"Good. They're all inescapably naïve and not worth my attention."

"Perhaps you would like my opinion-although it might count for nothing,"

"I'd be glad to have it anyway," he replied politely.

"These girls they've painted up the wrong picture between us, but I don't mind. You made my boring life look somewhat compelling this evening."

Up front and on stage the dazzling models elicited repeated applause from the audience. The ingenuity of the stage technicians provided spellbinding and constantly changing backdrops without the need for a curtain. Back by the drinking water cooler Stark leaned over, took a sip of water and said, "Level with me, Miss Reyes. What are you doing this evening after work?"

"Nothing, why?" JeZe Bella asked in a courteous tone.

"Good. Have dinner with me. A nice charcoal-broiled steak, will pick-up your spirits. Only, we'll have to meet there. I'm still on duty for two more hours."

"All right," she agreed reluctantly. "But where are we to meet?"

"I hope you can read my scribbled directions, I'm afraid they look bit hieroglyphic." He laughed looking so virile.

She watched him, spellbound, as he drew a map on the back of his paper cup. But something weird was happening in the way she so quickly shared his plans. Barry Stark turned to look at her one more time before departing.

"JeZe Bella, he's got to be the prettiest macho cop on Broadway," Ronnie Love said excitedly as more of the girls gathered around her.

"I have a rendezvous with him tonight," she admitted. "But I don't know if I'm going to keep this date."

"Well, everyone is entitled to a little fun now and then girl."

"You're right, Ronnie. I can't allow my conscience to spoil things for me,"

"JeZe Bella, he is so hot and sexy, does he have a twin?" Maria Torres said, "He caught more than my eye when he flashed me a seductive smile."

"Hey, maybe I can arrange to have my purse snatched next time." Dionne Norris joked as she pulled the blue wig jealously from her head.

"You girls sound like flips. Besides, you all said you'd come over tomorrow and help me move to my new condo apartment, remember?" JeZe Bella reminded them.

"Sorry, it's off now," Maria, replied. "So, you can make this cop tumble to your charms in the bedroom-like you've already planned."

"Is that what you think?" JeZe Bella asked with a mischievous smile on her heavily made-up face.

"I'm almost willing to believe you're capable as we all are!" Ronnie refrained.

"Don't be such a Bitch! Go on, all of you. I don't need any of your help," JeZe Bella retorted at her friends as they moved away laughing.

Elaine Gondi heard the muffled voice in tears, and pushed open the door. JeZe Bella slowly lifted her head as Elaine anxiously offered what comfort she could.

"Look honey, you can tell me to butt out, if you want to. But I heard the girls turn on you, and all over a date. Well, you can't let that keep you from the guy. So, hurry and get out of here before you miss him."

"But I'm not going, Elaine," JeZe Bella responded, with fake cheerfulness.

"Oh, come on now and fix your tear-stain face. You can't let them win, their jealous because Cherry Red happens to think you have a good chance to be the Agency's Model of the year and help land the Cover Girl contract."

"You are right, Elaine. I won't let them beat me down."

"That's my girl show some back-bone." She sounded conspiratorial.

"Okay. I won't be the object of pity," Jeze Bella confessed. Down the hall, the models pushed open the heavy metal exit door and found themselves out on the street. With each step, the noises of the street life grew louder. From a distance, a siren wailed with horrendous force that vibrated the heart strings. A moment later, Jeze Bella's figure emerged from the hotel's service entrance. Following the directions on the paper cup that Barry had given her, she drove for twenty minutes to the east side of town, to a steakhouse with a western atmosphere. Psyched-up Barry had an intensity she hadn't seen before. JeZe Bella senses violence and tenderness, without honor or illusions and all in moment her life

is brought to a point of reckoning. At first, she had rejected in her mind his suggestion that they meet for a late dinner but finds that compelling forces inside her have already taken on a will of their own. In his company she feels bathed in a vivid light and everything about her seems to sing vibrantly, was this the man of her dreams? She had looked at him with questioning eyes; maybe it was his combustible charm. Indelibly she drove into the bumpy parking lot behind the restaurant. Barry was early and stood waiting by the door, his face split into a wide grin. She lowered her heavily cosmetic eyes and then threw him a level gaze.

Inside the restaurant, he hung his warm leather jacket on a coat rack in the small lobby and then they walked through the doorway into a spacious room with a sawdust floor. Moving away from the rowdy bar, to the left of the room, sat a piano on an elevated stage. Directly behind them, Barry took note of the fact that there was no one present who knew him. Then, as he continued to glance around the room, JeZe Bella suddenly whispered in his ear.

"Do you come here often?" she asked in a soft purr.

"Sometimes," was all he said.

The aroma of smoked steak and mesquite wood from the fireplace filled the air around them. As she paused in front of a certain table, Barry made a curious remark. "I feel lucky tonight. You've just walked up to my favorite table." With that, he pulled back a chair for her with the tip of one leather boot.

"Oh, so you're one of those highly flexible individuals who always know exactly observed coyly. As she cotton halter. hat to say in any situation," JeZe Bella spoke, she caressed the folds of her white

Like a pair of wolves on the prowl, two city cowboys brushed past them, eyeing JeZe Bella. They seemed totally unaware of Barry's presence. The midnight rush hour was on. With one waitress and four waiters on the floor, the restaurant seemed short of help to handle the busy and hungry crowd.

Consequently, Barry raised his arm to attract the attention of his favorite waitress. After chatting with two other nightly regular customers, she came quickly and cleared off their table, spreading a fresh checkered tablecloth and leaving two menus.

"Sally, bring us a large cold pitcher of Coors beer?" Barry said then.

"Sure, Stark! As you can see it's a bit rowdy here tonight," Sally remarked over her shoulder as they laughed it off.

Downing half a glass of beer in a single gulp, Barry eyed his dinner companion. "That just hit the spot!" he sighed contentedly. "It feels good to relax after a day on my feet," she acknowledged.

"You wouldn't want my job either," Barry told her. "Take today---all on one city block. I'd kid-you-not, a rape, two burglaries and one mugging. Not to mention a load of paperwork that goes along with all the other complaints. But there's not a damn thing I can do about it. Especially the raped cases-none of the hookers want to prosecute."

JeZe Bella drew a deep breath at the very thought of what his day had entailed. "I guess you guys have it tough," she said. "I mean, I've been reading in the newspapers that the police are catching a lot of flak because of Black-lives'-matters and the fearsome killer "" cop."

"Yes, one of us is working things out his way. But then again, it's the scum backs or us," he said, and snatched up a handful of peanuts from a small bowl in the center of the table.

"Good grief, human blood is certainly not a deterrent," she gasped.

He paused for a moment before answering her. "Well, you can't feel what we do," he said at last. "I know I don't think I'll ever see a pension. I'm too fed-up and disgusted with the system to fight them all back."

Eyeing him curiously, JeZe Bella made no move. His green eyes held her in a golden silence.

"Been modeling long in town?" he asked then.

"Two years. I'm with the Cherry Red Modeling Agency."

"Cherry Red, what's that, party drinks?" he asked in an incredulous voice.

"Oh' no, Cherry Red was once a top model back in the '50s. Lipsticks nail polishes and cheek blushers-you know the whole bit. She always wore a particular shade of red, her trademark. She now runs her own agency," JeZe Bella concluded briskly.

"You speak of it as if it were only yesterday," he observed coolly.

"Well, she was the best, Barry. And she happens to think that I could be the Model of the Year. That means lots of magazine covers and commercials, of course. My photographer, Tony Savage, has had a lot to do with it. His camera work is way above all other photographers in the business."

"Do you really go for all this attention?" Barry asked then, as if he weren't sure, it was worth it.

JeZe Bella admitted candidly. "I could never be dissatisfied with my work and continue doing it. That isn't bragging. I'm just being realistic."

Barry nodded his head, eyes fixed on her body, she was drop dead gorgeous as delicate as a porcelain glass doll. She swallowed dismissing him, he realized her shyness and nervousness was part of her while watching intently, "You must be very good at turning and twisting on the cat walk?"

"I'm a professional, Barry!" she blushed, her lips were pink and full. His features were already imprinted with an expression, a dazzling innocent smile that caused her to smile back at him. Unashamedly as their eyes connected with a comforting chuckle. She never seen a cop so clean and breath taking in a navy-blue uniform.

As if reading her mind, he dropped a breath mint to his mouth. "I've always found all this extravagance a little disgusting?"

Jeze Bella looked at him with disagreeable expression suddenly defending her job, "It pays the rent, this kind of luxury."

"Yes, I guess you eat well, better than most of us." He winked.

"Barry, there's no penalty in that if you make the money and are happy."

"Yes, there is no disgrace in that." By now Barry's passion was based on more than desire and conquest he was highly attracted to her. It was madness how could he say to her the truth, that he was a married man. And nothing could interfere with his dedication to his job. A man who lives for the chase of the most wanted criminals who should be behind bars. He is tough and somewhat stubborn, even a bit obsessive in more ways than one. His justice is now for the thrill he feels. Knowing the law was on his trail particularly one Lieutenant Bloodworth, who has been watching his every move. But now his greater rush will be his lusty pursuit for this beautiful and young model. Who now tested his patience at the end of this day's work? Still never feeling exposed or unarmed with his hard-charging style of law enforcement accessorized by a black Glock on his hip, the guided missile for law and order on the streets. Just sitting close beside her he thought of himself a terrific guy. Who's been going to the gym twice a week to look perfect too-a-Tee in his police uniform.

On an enjoyable and gleefully first date, JeZe Bella did not know what to think of such a man. Most charming or a big asshole-definitely petulant and completely self-involved and rude at times. Yet he did not have to be likable to be so glistening and interesting as a two-dollar bill.

Soon their conversation was interrupted by a jubilant country singer. Who pounded on the piano keys, as people in the room began to clap with the tempo? Barry leaned forward and placing a hand behind her neck, and urged her to move toward him. When she did, he gave her a tender kiss on the cheek, which left her a little mystified and momentarily speechless. Then turning her head in a symbolic gesture of surrender, she listened to the music, knowing the compliment from his lips had meant something. The late evening begins on a high note but the naked truth, a seduction made easy moves quickly like a wolf on the hungry prowl. JeZe Bella Reyes made no move; his gleaming-colored eyes held her helplessly. After they had finished their dinner, she watched him pick-up the tab and then he led her out slowly. While other females eyed him momentarily her heart sank, his sexual and physical powers were invincible. When, he pressed his thighs to hers, interlacing her slender fingers with his own. Within his grip she trembled as his heavy metal badge pressed into her pouty breast.

"This is an excellent eating establishment. Thank you for inviting me here tonight," she said sincerely.

"Hey, maybe we'll take in a Broadway Show next time," he suggested tentatively.

"I don't suppose you happen to know what musical play would be the best to see."

"That depends," he said, searching.

"On what I might ask you?"

"On whether or not my card is up-to-date." With that, he pulled a card from his wallet that gave the weekly listings at each theater. "Well, a comedy would be fun don't you think?" She jested. "Indeed?"

"Yes." Sensing his eyes upon her, she blushed deeply but held his steady gaze.

"Then tell me, JeZe Bella, which one shall we see? Wicked, Jersey Boys, Aladdin or Lion King" he said playfully.

"You're so swank, Barry," she said with laughter brimming in her eyes.

"Thanks, but is that a yes to one of them?"

In the pursuit for amusement and entertainment, they stood close for a long moment, their ears taking in the street noises. To JeZe Bella, a now basic badge worshipper, Barry was a somewhat heroic figure against the dusky violet shadows-a cultural jewel with bloodshot eyes that sparkled as the flames of a fire.

"Are reading my you mind?" He asked solemnly.

"Possibly, and?" She said climbing into her roomy Ford Explorer with dark tinted windows.

"Wait! I've got to take a piss!" He shouted and jumped back behind the red truck.

"Barry, you've picked a fine time to take a leak!"

"Well beer has a way of always going through a guy's gut."

"Yes, by the sound of things!" she teased and then heard the back seat door being locked from behind as Barry dropped his *warm leather* jacket on the floor board beside them.

"Do you think we should?" she asked, reading the urgent message in his steamy eyes. "I mean, right here in this parking lot?" Even as she spoke, he was sliding over to her with his fly unzipped and his gun belt undone. "I was wondering what your underwear would say about you, Officer Stark!"

"In your analyzing did you think I wore any at all under this uniform by the way I'm hung and need some support?" He said pulling her skirt up.

JeZe Bella's arms reached out and her fingers ran slowly and smoothly through his short dark brown hair. She could feel every inch of his body pressed tightly to hers, as it forced her to give her breathless all.

His flesh turned warmer and harder as he moved slowly and sensuously. "I'm getting strong feelings over you," he vowed under his beer breath.

"Perhaps you are!" she teased back at him.

"You think I'm joking?" He snapped abruptly.

Sensing a new potential and power in her, JeZe Bella responds. in a coy, flirtatious manner, hinting broadly at her willingness to participate in a brief, frivolous tae-a-tae. Barry is obviously annoyed with her dismissal of his feelings as if she were party to many quick conquests. Her emotions are basically of a shallow superficial nature and that he has laid himself bare to the wrong female. Even so, he is determined to have his way with her, if only to regain a position of control. Without the burdensome complication of their mutual attraction, JeZe Bella Reyes's professional and personal life can be truly enviable in terms of present circumstances and future promise. Now at the peak of her career, she is a strong contender for model of the year award, and owing to her agency's acquisition of an exclusive cosmetic contract, her face will soon become the official trademark for their entire line of products. The other models at the Cherry Red Agency, where JeZe Bella is employed, are envious of her soaring career, and intrigued by her relationship with Barry Stark, given the opportunity to emulate her on any level. They would be hard pressed to choose between her professional success and her extraordinary charm with men.

Arriving at her place very tired she drew the blinds, hoping for a laid-back morning in the stillness of her bedroom. She then turns on the radio and in a sad mood listened to a song from Brendetta Davis entitled, (I can't make it without him). JeZe Bella now had built a life of total solitude. She had entered Barry Stark's universe and he to her was unlike no other man she'd had ever known and was now forever a captive. This abnormal attraction came from his style which was laconic. But like some great virtuoso's command of song, dance or music she would follow him to the end of time. He was a small gem a diamond in the ruff. She found him so striking and affecting as any villain capable of larceny and blackmail. It would not matter now, they were a pairing she though, for her this was no hilarious romp in a hayloft or thankless servitude but a rallying cry of loneliness. Soon his surprising sexual cell phone call shattered her thoughts by his threatening voice on the other end – but her irresistibly curiosity finds herself entangled in the trauma of this intense, sinuous man never not knowing who he truly was. Because Barry did not play by the rules, he was a life-changer. With implications far beyond what anyone could ever anticipate. Too handsome to be trusted - rubbing his cold dark brown hair with both hands was something he did and she loved seeing him doing it.

The overshare of Barry Stark was no page out of history. He is more richly revealing with a will and determination to succeed against all odds. He was the approaching storm like the clouds over New York City. That he only knows so well, where revenge and ambition go with love, sex and greed. His unbridled drive for justice was just as ruthless and went from the surface streets of Broadway Boulevard too hell and back. When this gutsy model defies her humble beginnings and who now takes the glamorous world of the modeling business by storm. When a turbulent love affair with a rogue cop. Who will eventually find themselves caught up in a series of dramatic and sinister events that test their resolve?

SCREAMING HEADLINES
CHAPTER 3

JeZe Bella's immediate emotional quest is played out against a backdrop of violent and senseless murders that presently plague the teeming New York City skyline. Seeking to calm her indecisive heart, the shadows and threats from without take on a decidedly more ominous tone. Screaming headlines and hourly bulletins attest to the violence that has been unleashed in the city. There was cause for concern-even alarm-as the murders mount and no real suspects are taken into custody. The next morning, at a local businessman's brunch, NYC -Metro Police chief Abraham addressed the group about crime and the News Media. Having approached the podium in his finest blues, he did not care to be quoted as saying precisely what he thought. "It's hard to imagine seriously, that I have a psycho cop on the force who is desperate, foolish and destructive, but I also feel that the press deserves some criticism. They don't always do the best job and that goes for the
Times and other daily newspapers people here today!"

"Chief, are you referring to an editorial in this morning's paper? Marsh's blasting comments?" A political observer shouted in the back row.

"Sometimes malice has a wanton disregard for the truth." The Chief retaliated immediately. "Everyone should be closely scrutinized. The Press, for one, takes a highly negative view of whatever Public Officials do. They always publish the negative side of any decisions by turning them around and saying something different." The Chief sounded frustrated at this point, as he wipes the sweat from his neck.

"Such as this morning's story by an unnamed source saying that you were apparently on your way out!" A female reporter, Molly insinuated in order to get an official answer.

"I'm not leaving!" The Chief told them amid the rumors. "Whatever the source, they are not from the Police Department. For the record, the Police Commissioner called early, after reading the article, and assured me that everyone in the Department was behind me one hundred percent, and would say so if necessary."

"It still remains; New York's detective elite have no line on one of their own." Observed gruff old Bea Strick the special envoy sent by MSNBC. She was the top woman to control the net work's vast machinery, a trouble-shooter answerable to no one. Her very presence left a sting as did her questions. By one public reading through the newspapers or watching her polished expertise report on television.

"There is a special investigative unit on the case," the Chief explained. "I can't say any more on the damn matter." Red faced with anger, he knew she couldn't be put off by any evasive answers but feared the FBI would soon step in, over the mounting pile of Law Suits and Peace Bonds against the Metro Precinct. As things don't always reach the majestic heights that the police officers were to aspire to. But someone went for broke as a man obsessed. Astonishingly not finding the power to resist going rogue as a lethal assassin. Who somehow had been drawn into a killing game?

It was late morning almost lunch time like a kindergarten class the NYPD cops on patrol did it with black batons and silver handcuffs and were out in full force. In close contact with the public the fleet was being used as a recruitment tool for their division. They were going through a motorcycle inspection and drills as a crowd gathered around them. With their cell phone cameras and videos that would soon go viral.

"Move on people, there is nothing to see here!" Sergeant, Romero strongly commanded.

While a squad of new Harley Davidson motorcycles stood in a row side by side military style against the street curb and heaps of garbage. The Metro's young helmeted police officers sat straddled on them. With dark glasses and their arms fully crossed over their chests, looking straight ahead. Watching a group of juvenile delinquents on the crosswalk going pass them.

Flipping their middle finger and trying to provoke the officers of the law by yelling at them. "What do we want? Dead pigs under a white sheet!" For they were not the kids next door.

"Get going doofuses before I cuff all of you and take you in for littering and disturbing the peace." Barry Stark said snarky but with a chin out grin.

"Serg! These hoody punk offenders are so messed-up," Officer, Brent Barrett said.

"Excuse them, we still have freedom of speech in this country. They're just pricks and drop-outs." The sergeant reasoned.

This was all in a day's work for the police department as Barry Stark sat back, day dreaming of JeZe Bella Reyes. Before he ever got on his right knee again, he was sure the answer would be yes. He had his dream girl; it was all or nothing. Everything he found in her was born the night they met. JeZe Bella was truly all he ever wanted and this was too good to be true. If not for his wife Anne that stood between them. Suddenly, Barry now stepped on a cigarette with his long *warm leather* boot. Spitting on the dirty pavement over the smelly odor of the garbage piles on the city's sidewalks. While the Mayor fights to maintain the city's sanctuary status, no matter what it takes. Creating growing problems and trouble for the police, immigration and customs enforcement (ICE). In the heated conditions the squad of Police Officers rived up their motorcycles and took to the street scene one by one. Brent and Barry paired off down the avenue of smut and lost souls that crossed the Broadway Boulevard of broken hearts and human wreckage.

THE APARTMENT
CHAPTER 4

IT WAS SHORTLY after 10:00 a.m. standing right below the bright brass antique ceiling fan, Jeze Bella had been preoccupied. She was looking at the decorative wallpaper that she had selected with the help of a small budge. "This jungle design is rather interesting," she thought, "Even though the paper is too cheap for words." Glancing about the cozy room, she felt that the new lease for the modern condo apartment was like a dream come true. When the doorbell rang, "That must be the furniture," she said aloud. As she glanced out the balcony window, and saw that a moving van had backed-up to the curb below. JeZe Bella eagerly pranced to the door so that she could watch the men unloaded her furniture. Soon three burly men came up with a Baby Grand piano. She couldn't help wondering about her new surroundings as the men unrolled the area rug and continued to transport furniture into the room.

"Miss, don't just stand there. Tell us where you want this damn stuff."

"It's very confusing, isn't it?" JeZe Bella said. "I mean—I'll probably move it ten times before I decide exactly where I want everything to go."

The man who had spoken gave her a long, disgusted look. "For this I had to work on my day off," he grumbled. "I should 'a said to hell with it."

"Relax, Gil. Don't pay him any mind," the other man said. "By the way, my name is Teddy." Teddy was chewing on the end of an unlighted cigar as he spoke. "Gil is a stickler, who would rather work at the warehouse in Brooklyn.

JeZe Bella's shoulders gave a gentle shrug, "Oh, I don't mind, Teddy. Really, my father used to yell at me the same way."

"Sure, is a nice place you've got here."

"You should have seen the tenement I came out of. A real rat's nest! They had entries and escape hatches you wouldn't believe. At least now I won't have to worry about my clothes getting eaten or roommate's barrowing my dresses."

"You were lucky to get out. Who needs that kind of aggravation?" Teddy asked with a ring of humor in his voice.

After the movers left, JeZe Bella commenced moving chairs and tables around, occasionally stopping to push a wisp of black hair back on her forehead.

When the doorbell rang again, the caller was Barry Stark. "I thought you might need an extra pair of hands," he volunteered.

"Thanks anyway, but the furniture has been put in place, and the dishes have all been unpacked and I just finished putting them away."

In the romanticism of the afternoon, Barry dropped his helmet, *warm leather* jacket and a pair of gloves on the white cane back chair.

Glancing over to the piano, he saw her glamorous image in a large metal picture frame. Caught in an emotional web, Barry sat right down on the piano bench and played with a technical brilliance that seemed to come naturally to him. In the highest thumb position, he flawlessly executed double hand over hand stops with superb sensitivity, but never once flaunted his talent, merely interpreting the strange prelude.

Spontaneously, there was a round of hand-clapping from JeZe Bella at the conclusion of the private concert for one.

"That's was simply breathtaking! What was it from?" she asked, with sweeping emotion.

"Verdi's overture to the opera of Aida."

"Well, this is probably the most beautiful feeling I've ever experienced at the hands of another talents. Barry, you have the mark of a great artist," she sighed, in this surprising moment.

"Maybe once. I was sixteen when I gave it up. That was after my parents both died in an automobile accident on New Year's Eve," he said, in underlined meditative thought. "Then I went to live with my grandmother."

"I'll bet you didn't take a lot of tending to," she responded in a wistful voice.

"She used to hug me and tell me how much I meant to her. I could not fight her kindness. Yes, my ups and downs are undeniable. She died while I was serving in the Iraq war."

"I guess we all have our emotional scars." JeZe Bella smiled sadly. "Are you sure there isn't anything I can do?" He asked, abruptly changing the subject of battle he soon forgets.

"I'm sorry, Barry. I'd offer to make you lunch, but I'm exhausted!"

"No problem. I'm good at fixing my own lunch. I hope you like hamburgers," he said, as he started shaping the ground beef into little cakes.

JeZe Bella soon felt better and started to peel the potatoes so they could make some French fries.

After they'd eaten their lunch and drank a pitcher of ice tea, they did the dishes and then put them away.

"You look like you're ready to lie down for a while," Barry suggested then.

"Yes, I am. But I'm warning you---no acts of pleasure."

"Trust me," he said, and followed her into the bedroom, where they both undressed and lay down together.

Listening to his laugh, she thought how manly and thrilling his voice was, as he gathered her in his arms and pressed hot kisses to her soft red lips. His embrace was powerful, even a little ruthless, and banished all other thoughts from her mind. In a state of pleasant drowsiness, she realized that a great deal of time had slipped away by the time exhaustion finally overtook her. But he demanded more sex and still more, until finally she began to cry.

He went to turn on the shower tap as he stood naked, so tall and physical, "What are you gaping at?"

"Nothing, please go."

"For a minute, I thought you'd changed your mind," he said, snapping on his tighty-whitey-briefs with a wide grin and a wink. She manufactured a smile, "you wish!"

"I heard there was a prowler in the area. Look, lock up, I'll see you," he said, then dressed and went out the door with a nasty swagger.

She appeared at the window a number of times, peering out in various directions. But all that moved below on the pavement was a lone taxi driver, searching impatiently for his riders.

Barry Stark was the angel from some hell and the man who she worshiped at the altar and the very ground his feet walked on. Even though her tear stain makeup in the mirror told her, he was wrong for her. Never thinking god would ever put such a man like that to walk the earth.

UNSYMPATHETIC AND CRUEL
CHAPTER 5

AFTER A FEW weeks sensing that her alliance with Barry has gone beyond the role of merely entertaining a lover, JeZe Bella seeks to break the bond and finds him totally unsympathetic and cruelly possessive. He taunts her by insisting he is too much for her and by accusing her of playing around with the photographer.

"Is this what you call getting in touch with your masculine side, Barry? "She screamed most predictable.

'Ha! Ha!" He shouted back, "Look you didn't lose anything to me!" he retorted in a way that was designed to make her feel cheap. Mounting his motorcycle and finally leaving on the heels of a disdainful prediction that she'll soon come back snooping after his ass. Turning her head so he did not see, as she fought back the tears, there exists in JeZe Bella's own heart the dreadful suspicion that he may well be right. Still there is something else about Barry that disturbs her even more. Something too direct, too intense about him for her own taste, she dislikes the manner in which he is able to open and close his personality over people, making them either the most important or the least important person in his life. Outside of herself, there exists for Barry yet another strong bond in of his partner on their same beat, Officer Brent Barrett. They have shared a special friendship and protected one another through any number of lives---threatening incidents. They shared a mutual contempt for their supervisors, Police Chief Abraham, and the somewhat over-zealous Police Lieutenant Bloodworth. They also disdain the more highly publicized side of their police work, preferring to do their job, and avoid whenever possible the media hype surrounding the more sensational case in which they are involved.

STANDING ORDERS
CHAPTER 6

THIS MORNING WALKING into the busy police headquarters, Barry said to Brent, "He's a pain in the pit of my pretty ass"

"A choice observation, pale," Brent replied as a trail of eyes from the office staff followed them to the door of Police Chief Abraham's office. It was precisely one minute to nine o'clock. They were flawlessly punctual. Scanning the print in the manila folder report with the face of a jurist, the chief still smelled of his morning breakfast-eggs and pork sausage. As he emptied his cup of straight black coffee, Barry and Brent quizzically looked at one another, and then turned right on command.

The Chief sat occupying a big wooden chair, shuffling more papers in front of him. As his eyes looked up, he studied the face of both his officers, and then took them on as he shifted his three-hundred-pound bulk around in his squeaking chair. "Well Stark! I see you've denied any wrongdoing and blamed this scuffle on the drunk."

"Yes, Sir!" Stark spoke up.

"Don't be so pompous, "Supervisor Ted Huck of Internal Affairs said as he walked in late. "Your little scuffled resulted in the hospitalization of a fifty-year-old vet and another lawsuit in the making!"

"There will be no department squabbles here this morning. "The Chief stated firmly. "This is only a hearing into the matter, Huck. Please sit down."

"And I say there is a great deal of insensitivity on the force today, with everyone doling out their own brand of our Justice," Huck retorted somewhat cynically.

"You may continue, Officer Stark."

"I deny hitting, kicking, punching or choking the gentleman. I just put a restraining hold on him in order to handcuff him. Officer Barrett can back me up."

"That's correct, chief! That's when the man became irate and attempted to strike Officer Stark and take his gun." Brent was quick to go along for he didn't want any resentment from Barry and his co-workers at the Metro Precinct.

"Some wrestling occurred while I tried to handcuff him. It never would have happened if he hadn't attempted to strike me in the face."

"That's actually what precipitated the whole thing."

"All right, you both can go now. There will be no disciplinary action taken on you, Stark, due to Officer Barrett's acknowledged observation in evidence," Chief said with a wink and smile.

Both Officers left with a lump in their throats.

"Look, Huck-I have more to worry about than these two bad boys," the chief sneered. "They're just on the edge with all the bad press we're getting from the Black Lives group and the DC Attorney General." He leaned back in his chair and rolled a thick cigar between his fat fingers.

"Now look here, Abraham. We need more body cameras on these men. This Stark is totally capable and determinedly ruthless. Just the same, I'd keep an eagles' eye on him and his buddies."

"Yes, these young blooded warriors make me nervous," the chief admitted, with his blue eyes ablaze, and clutching the incriminating report in the folder.

Coming away from Metro P.D. after giving tainted information, Barry and Brent looked at each other, offended, victimized and hostile. "What does it take to keep a career, Barry?"

"We've got to do whatever it takes to sustain it, Brent!" Never thinking what their reaction might be, they chuckled to a same minded conclusion.

DUTY ON THE PROWL
CHAPTER 7

RIDDING THEIR MOTORCYCLES through the city, it felt like a descent into a steamy Hell. Somewhat in a daze Barry found what he was looking for as they turned the street corner. He spotted JeZe Bella's Red Ford Explorer Park on the curb next door to a fashionable boutique beside a flower cart displaying an assortment of freshly cut flowers wrapped in brightly colored. tissue papers.

"Wait here, Brent. I'll only be ten minutes. I want to say hi, to the model I was telling you about!"

"You got it, boss!" Brent said with a sharp salute.

Adding to the loud music were the fashion reporters and Elaine Gondi on the microphone inside the Hat Box Boutique.

"The key to it all is choosing the right accessories and hats. That will add a little magic to your p.m. hours. When you have a certain man on your mind, ladies, go for high impact and pull out all the strings. Gilt, glimmer in the excitement of sequins in a tight crochet sweater shirt and harm pants."

Onward, Jeze Bella stepped out of the bright spotlight. She was in exceptional form, making a few key turns and poses as another model quickly stepped into the limelight.

Barry slowly strode toward JeZe Bella, time to escape; her face was like an angry mask as she pushed through a small cluster of people to the dressing room and slipped behind a dressing screen. Amid the sounds of female voices that cut through, Barry held out to her a bouquet of soft pink roses.

"Can't it wait?" she entreated, not wanting the girls behind her to get an earful.

"What jive is this? You mad?" his voice had a stinging hiss.

"Barry, you're thought-provoking," she said with a shake of her head. "And you think nothing of it."

"JeZe Bella, I didn't come here to hear any of your fucking lip."

"For God's sake, watch your langue! Don't start making waves, I'm on a job! You just can't barge in here and air your dirty laundry about me like nothing has happened between us. Barry, you have a heart made of stone. It's over when it's all over, don't you know when we've struck out?"

"Then don't give me the runaround," he answered, pacing back and forth.

"Look, pig! I tried to be nice to you. Now, if you don't want to end up the bigger fool, you'll just leave like I asked you to, because this girl from Puerto Rico is through talking."

Unexpectedly, with attacking words, Barry painted his theories in loud echoes over Elaine Gondi's voice and shocked the hell out of the audience of woman up front.

"You, oddball, get out of here! I hate you!" JeZe Bella screamed as she tossed the bouquet of roses at his feet.

"That's gratitude bitch! but you'll soon come back begging me for some dick." Barry left through the rear exit, complaining idly to himself.

"I demand to know what in hell is going on back here," Elaine said running back into the dressing room.

"It serves JeZe Bella right," Maria Torres observed coolly. "Stark, cop criticized her for being glib with him." the

"You must think he is a joy and a privilege to have around-----well, he's not."

"Oh, can't it, the both of you." Elaine clutched her hands. "JeZe Bella, how did he know you were here?"

"He called the agency, how else?"

"Maria, get out front. We still have a show to wrap up, even if it is spoiled," Elaine ordered.

"So much for the police of N.Y.C. Right, JeZe Bella?" Maria smirked with a cat-like walk.

JeZe Bella could only wave a hair brush at her. The meter outside had just run out, so did her luck. JeZe Bella Reyes had been given a ticket in the form of a five hundred dollar fine for a parking violation. When a short time later she waltz out and saw Barry and his partner go to a secluded corner of the busy street, lean against the building and watch sourly as she tore the ticket in half, driving off.

"Why, that stupid cunt!" Barry yelled.

"Woo! Cool off Barr!!!" Brent said, casting a long shadow, "you don't look so hot buddy?"

Yeah! Yeah! What a Bitch?" Barry paced up and down.

"Obviously, you're unhappy with her? I find it strange what's this all about, Barry?" Brent begged as he stepped in front of him.

All of sudden, he was asked to tackle the whole issue in the dead of heat of this high noon sun. The air became sweltering on the hot asphalt street. Instantly, wide streaks of red, yellow and blue flashed in front of Barry's eyes. Confused, he wanted to vomit.

"Barr! Relax! You don't look so hot." Brent implored. Before he could respond, he bent over in a fit of deep convulsive coughs that continued for several minutes.

"I'd better get you to the emergency room at Merriam's Clinic?"

Looking like a case of heat exhaustion, Barry looked puzzled, hallucinating from the heat. "It's not all that bad, Brent. A good sweat offers certain gratifications."

"You're all warmth today, buddy." Brent quickened onto the motorcycle.

"All the same the ungrateful and disrespectful bitch is breaking the law. Well, I'm not going to sit around and let the slut get away with it on my beat. JeZe Bella Reyes is so typical and doesn't know who she is messing with." He said with syndical and dark enthusiasm.

"Sure, whatever you say, Stark."

"Brent, don't tell your wife. I don't want Anne to find out about any of this." Barry requested from him.

"Sure. Like I said, whatever you say." Brent soon becomes aware of Barry's infatuation with this JeZe Bella Reyes, but initially believes or even hopes that she is a passion that will quickly spend itself. His opinion of JeZe Bella ranges from a state of general indifference to a vague sort of dislike. Even without knowing the model, he feels she has the capability of influencing Barry in some detrimental way. But he keeps his thoughts to himself until he begins to sense a condition of inner torment in his best friend. Far from hearing more of Barry's steamy romps, naively, when he feels it is finally safe to speak his mind, Brent suggests that JeZe Bella is not worth Barry's time and trouble and notices a new impatience. In his surly quality and reaction, the refusal to confide in his friend, or even discuss the matter of JeZe Bella. Barry dismisses Brent's attitude in terms of his own personal disapproval of extra-marital affairs, and the pain that inevitably results from them. Barry is married and the father of two young sons, and having always professed to be the proverbial family man, is suddenly behaving in a manner Brent finds totally out of character. Further, the pressures of his clandestine involvement seem to be taking on a physical toll, to the extent that Barry occasionally suffers the effects of certain devitalizing spells for which there are not any rational explanation. Dehydration, Barry insists on those days when the temperature is soaring, although he finds other reasons when it's not a sore point, within the cle of his own best buddies. The following night, the delicious smell of chicken was in the air. When Barry, half-drunk, finally stumbled into the dining room of his home, as his *warm leather* jacket hit the floor he spotted the table, elaborately set, and a serving platter piled high with succulent chicken, North Carolina style. But before his wife Annie could pitch in to serve him a portion, he grabbed her arm and twisted it as she caught the smell of his sweaty body.

"Just a moment, I didn't ask for chicken." His emotions surfaced.

"Chicken," she mumbled. "You crave chicken, remember?"

"It's after eight. I'm not very hungry." His exhaustion had taken over.

"I guess it isn't any use in me griping about it then." There was no remorse, just an antagonizing feeling she felt in his mood.

"Where are Michael and Patrick?"

"After a few beers you remembered you have two sons! Why, they've been fed hours ago and put to bed with the TV still on. Barry, you haven't forgotten what day this is?"

"Annie, don't play these silly games with me. You know I can't stand it when you do." His face could break hers with a single glance of his burning blood-shot eyes.

"I was right. You really have forgotten. But then, maybe you'd like me to think you also don't care about us anymore," she argued sadly.

"You mean it's our wedding anniversary again," he stated as the tears formed around her blue eyes. She was wearing a new pink satin negligee with small white dots under her white apron. He hated seeing her in that tantalizing way crowded up against the arm chair.

"Yes, six years is a long time, Barry, I'm just glad you're all right, I was a bit worried after hearing what happened to you today."

"Oh, fuck! From Constance, no doubt! Brent, my best friend couldn't keep his mouth shut." His face got a little pale as she watched him closely. Eyeing his wife of many years he had bad feelings and emotions building-up inside. But it was no paying proposition. While her friends and other woman flattered him by their interest in him. Still he was considered quite a catch and all their bullshit he had to shrug-off. But would he be standing when it was all over? With them all was in his mediate thoughts.

"What's the good in complaining? She is his wife, Barry. Most spouses tell each other everything. Besides, I do have a right to know if you won't tell me," Annie lamented.

"Oh' hell! Don't leave me hanging. What else did she have to gossip about?" he glanced at her nervously, his fingers fumbling inside his pant pockets.

"Only that she is on this year's Halloween committee. Barry, she needs volunteers. Naturally, I said we'd be happy to help."

Barry felt like there was more, and wanted to punch out his frustration on the wall. "Naturally!" He said, walking away to preserve the peace.

Reprising her feelings that offered little solace, Annie turned and blew the long candlesticks out. From their golden candelabra, they burned up the oxygen with a vanilla-scented aroma. Snapping out of all he had been thinking, Barry was tired, dirty and needed to shave. He ran under the cold icy shower and soak off the stinking arm pit sweat. Moments later, he was shaved and dried down. Then he wrapped himself in a big white cannon towel and went to the kitchen for his nightly cold Coors beer, finding the glass plate of chicken still warm in the refrigerator. He chewed on the drumstick and seeped his beer as he walked down the hall barefooted. Along the way, he stopped to glance into the boy's room, where Annie stood, tucking them tightly under the plaid covers.

In the silence, there was a tinkle of the wind chimes outside the window. It had been an unusually mild autumn since the beginning of October. Now, in the privacy of their bedroom, Barry lay sprawled, face down, on the queen bed. He always slept in the nude.

Annie's hair was loose, and parted in the middle. She enjoyed the gentle, romantic feeling underlined by the warm touch of Russian musk oil on Barry's freshly scented body. It inspired a delicate awaking in her like a blooming lily.

"Barry, do you remember when we fell in love?"

"There was a time when I thought that was the only thing in life. But memories are a strange thing, or perhaps I'm more realistic now."

On the heels of this bad joke, her fond, unhappy eyes drifted away as she had tried to fondle him but he would not respond. He looked tired, through his imposing eyes, for he could hardly keep them open.

"What's wrong, Barry? Why must you drink yourself into unconsciousness every night lately?"

"For Christ's sake, nothing's wrong. Agh!"

"Barry, you opened your mouth just now as if you were going to say something more, then thought better of it. Everything takes a tremendous effort and it's hardly worth the trouble I go through for you," she said, crying as their eyes met.

Suddenly, he leaned forward absently, politely as her shoulder rose and took a mock bite of her bare flesh. It was a kind of joking flirtation. "I was only joking. Well, half-joking. But joking aside, I must explain to you Annie. My stomach—I got a pain in my gut."

His fixed gaze did not shift.

"How does it feel when it hurts?"

"Like a stabbing pain but really sharp."

"You're as pale as a ghost," she whispered. "Which side? It could be appendicitis."

"Don't look so fearful."

"Can I get you bicarbonate?"

"No nothing. Please, I feel it letting up now."

"Shush, shush. Okay, try and relax a bit more," she said, fixing the pillow and blanket about him.

All he could do was to roll over with a thundering hard on, as his mind silently fathomed JeZe Bella's dim, rosy breasts and the dark patch between her shapely long legs. The light that came through the window was nothing more than the starry sky.

More than ever Barry felt estranged from his marriage with all the unresolved issues. His private past not only has kept them apart and clouded his days in a high-stress job as he faces dark and very violent incidents. With no chance to regain his lost innocents he once had. There couldn't never be a reconciliation between them nor would he dare to breath a word of his conspiracy of silence that was buried deep in the heart. An evil that had been festering for some years. That was the target placed on his back and of his own making. He could only sigh knowing what fate had in store for him. With no precognition or psychic abilities, he paused knowing he was damn -scared and yielded more than he bargained for the agenda he refused to trust. For some years Barry was filled with unshakable visions in his head. Laying in the darkness of their bedroom there was a blind panic and desperation toward the invite to the arms of the angel of death. Barry hadn't written off the troubling images in his mind night after night. Suddenly he had awoken screaming from a plaguing nightmare. He tried to relate the never-ending dream to his wife. "Anne, please listen to me." He asked in a cold sweat. "It was an explosive day there was Humvees tearing across the Iraq sand fields behind me but I ignored them there was just too much going on in my head. I did not know how much longer I could stand in my moist socks and boots. Stumbling around all my efforts were a big waste. I almost gave up the urge to cry in the sweltering sun with as many soldiers in marine uniforms coming toward me. Dizzy and nauseated I avoided getting run over. There were voices and screams around me, whoever had been in the Humvee seemed to be following my ass! I couldn't even think straight anymore. When they pulled me in through an open door? My movements were a little sluggish and very unsteady. Then I collapsed onto the floor board, I was trapped and could not be forced to stand-up again. While the pain erupted in my head like an alarm clock that was all I remember. When I woke-up I peeked around the room. It was a hospital, white lights on the ceiling, it was some kind of tech medical room. Anne looks at me! For the next few months, I was in a sprawling barrack's complex playing soccer. Are you okay? A team player asked.' I said, 'my only problems are not visible.' He pointed to my head and smiled and turned his head back the game as a big wall of dust hung over the playing field. mug stopped me again and said, 'your body looks so athletic?" "That's me!' I answered rolling my green eyes at him. When the memories of a pale faced kid with braces from grade school came over me. But suddenly, I was given my papers and discharged from the military with PTSD. That's always how my recurring dream ends as I wake-up in our bed all wet." The

"Barry it's time you put all these bad dreams and memories aside. And stop wakening your kids with those horded screams." Anne replied, rolling over on her side of the bed with a fetal yawn turning the night lamp off. "Enough is enough!"

Barry then sat up in the darkness of the bedroom and was blindsided by his growing feelings for JeZe Bella but his wife was going to be something to contend with. Was the clock running out for his wife Anne? Maybe he'd just put a pillow over her face and hold it down to the last and final breath instead of strangling the life out of her. Leaving his DNA with that in mind. Feeling a cold chill his first thought, how to get rid of her body, there wouldn't be anything to clean up - his mind was whirling with manic thoughts. The truth be told it would be troublesome in what was less than the blink of his green eyes as he rolled over and went back to sleep. With everything coalescing around Anne, was she in the thick of the woods? She had no idea of it as she slept.

THE SCARLET DRESS
CHAPTER 8

THE MORNING DRIZZLE had long since stopped. Breezing in twenty minutes late, Jeze Bella had been carrying her raincoat around and was glad to throw it on the first coat rack she saw.

"Good morning, Elaine."

"Hum," she objected, holding a Xerox copy of an important file account.

"You're a little tight-lipped today. How's come?"

Temporarily distracted, Elaine put her pen down and swiveled around in her chair. "And why not, JeZe Bella, dear? I have to reshuffle some of our best secretaries around."

"A real pity, reducing the office staff, I mean."

"Well, there isn't any help for it. I've got my orders from the top. The economy, I'm afraid, affects us too. So, you' better hurry and change, we have big buyers waiting in the tea room to see one of our still reliable client's collections."

JeZe Bella took note and hastily retreated back to the fitting room.

"You call this a ball gown? Well, do you. Simon?" she screamed at the top of her lungs.

"But Maria, it's only an informal modeling of Francis Knight's New Year's Eve collection."

"And what do I care? All she is now is a name want-to-be. Here, take it off me before I rip it to pieces." She was being unnecessarily difficult.

"Someone has to model this scarlet dress!"

Pausing for a moment in the midst of the commotion, JeZe Bella stuck her head inside the door curiously.

"Give it her!" Maria suggested immediately. "The color is suited more to her since she isn't so particular these days." At that, she turned and started to redden her own lips.

"Maria, why must you always make trouble for everyone? Simon, please put the dress behind my screen," JeZe Bella immediately suggested.

"Trouble!" Maria sneered. "Listen to the soul of courtesy. The one I know who is dating a married man."

"Liar, where do you know this from?"

"Isa Radlett, the nigger that works as a singer at the Parrot Club."

"You're a mass of prejudices, aren't you? Well Maria, so much thought, and so little feelings." Simon interjected.

"Listen, she and Barry had a thing going over a year ago. I was at the club's bar talking with some of my friends. About this playboy cop, you know how he appears and disappears. Well, she overheard me say Barry Stark. So, she walked over and said, 'Small world'."

"Hilarious, isn't it?" JeZe Bella said a trifle bitterly. "I guess I knew all along. He does not wear a wedding-ring so I never wanted to ask. Now you've got something to crow about, haven't you, Maria?"

"I'm truly sorry, JeZe Bella. But everyone is always making a fuss over you. Someone had to knock you off that marble pedestal." "Okay, Maria. You said what you wanted to say. I've got the message. I've fallen from grace and God."

"It's all much ado about nothing if you ask me." Simon said, coming into the conversation for the second time. JeZe Bella was glum and then silent. He walked over to her maintaining his cool. Because egos were so explosive in an atmosphere of this kind, he felt it was best to set an opposite example. "You know the old saying, "The minute you go against intuition, you're digging your own grave."

"Oh, Simon---I'm devastated! No, I'm in love with this cop." Misty-eyed, she betrayed her feelings. "I was going to forgive him today if he called. Fool that I am, I almost threw my birth control pills away."

"Have some coffee with me. I've got a whole fresh pot on."

"Thanks, Simon. It's nice to know I have a friend but first help, me with this red dress. I really feel the part of a Jezebel," she said remembering Maria's odd comments.

"JeZe Bella, you're not going to make a production of it?"

"And why not, she's sure to broadcast it around."

"Lady, you're a pretty entertaining kook!" as he blurted this out, the other models started wandering into the fashion fitting room.

To stupefied and left senseless to face his less-than-perfect person and what he suddenly become in her mind. For she was in a slow-motion free fall crisis and felt dirty and ridiculously bogged down in a romantic triangle of truth and lies.

GUILT AND DECEPTION
CHAPTER 9

BARRY FEELS CONSTRAINED by the mutual burdens of guilt and deception. Throughout their married life, his wife Annie has immersed herself in good Christian habits, representing in his mind some paragon of virtue with whom it is difficult or even impossible to identify. Annie is a woman who freely embraces love but has a poor understanding of lust. She cannot equate the two emotions and is frequently repelled by the baser side of her husband's sensual nature. At the most inopportune times, she reminds him of important dates he has forgotten, anniversaries, birthdays and commemorations of events that seem actually more important to her than the events themselves. Annie is able to provoke him into sudden, impulsive acts, and Barry frequently storms out of the house in order to avoid what he views as her insufferable self-righteousness and thoroughly maddening logic. Still, Barry is plagued by the inner certainty that the quality of his wife's moral character, even without a trace of passion, is infinitely superior to that of his clandestine love, who continues to taunt him with her, you can't be real except my mercurial personality.

The unknowingly, the presence of JeZe Bella Reyes in Barry's life increases the distance between Annie and himself, a fact of reality that both puzzles and actively distresses her world. She berates him for his after hour drinking with buddies, who cause him to drink more, and suffers silently as he continues to pull away from her. Threatened, Annie becomes more acutely aware of his withdrawal, she attempts to rekindle an earlier closeness through her own subtle means. With hair let loose around her shoulders, she invites certain reminiscences of the past by staging a warm, intimate scene in the present. "Barry, you never use to turn me away when we first got married? "She asked, by way of confessing to a delicate stirring inside herself.

"Can't you see I am tried, Annie, when I think of little else between us." He counters. "But your memories are things from the past. Through these few years, feelings change there is kids in the relationship to keep us busy now. And we should be more realistic now!" he stated with a lump in his throat.

Annie's disappointment is clearly reflected in her eyes. Inevitably, she resigns herself to his rejection of her, although the question of why remains.

The next week, the New York P.D. volunteers turned out in full force to build the annual Halloween haunted house. With a little creative chaos, no one was idle for very long. Even the wives were working and laughing. With less than a few days to go, the place was in total disorder, what with the sawing, hammering and painting that continued at a frantic pace. Some of the men would pause periodically and yell coarse language back and forth. They shouted over the sounds of a football game in progress on a portable TV screen in one corner of the room.

"Say what, another fucking touchdown!"

"Come on, Miami Dolphins. Knocked on their asses."

"Hey man, who in the hell's side are you on?"

"That's right!" another shouted.

"Bullshit, I don't give a damn about the fucking home team," came a brawling reply.

"You suck man, because the New York Jets will take this one."

"Oh, screw all of you. Miami will win or I'll buy all of you a keg of beer."

"You're on!" everybody cried in unison.

Along the wide hall, two of the officer's wives were painting big ugly black bats on the coarse brick wall. Meanwhile, four others hung torn curtains on the dirty, dusty old windows facing the street below.

Among a small group of meddlesome ladies, Annie and best friend, Constance sat, busily carving jack-o-lanterns out of a dozen or so large orange pumpkins atop a rickety old table.

"Sonya, pass me another pumpkin."

"There you go."

"Annie, do you want any more help?"

"No, but thanks."

"Jessica, when was the last time you had sex? I mean, adulterated with some hunk." The question was asked to add a note of levity to their mood.

"Sonya, I haven't. Not lately. Pass me another pumpkin, please."

"Jessica, you don't impress me. It's too bad that you have such a nice husband and you cheat on him."

Their laughter was clouded over by Constance's disapproval. She had put on an icy face as the air went suddenly chilly.

"You're so straight. I realize we haven't taken the same path, but I wasn't always like this vulgar. But we can't always be so refined."

"I find that terribly hard to believe, but excuse me now. I have to go see how the others wives are doing, coming Annie?"

Not a word dropped from Annie's still lips.

"Why, That So-and-so." This irritated Sonya considerably.

"You really want to know something? She would make a good witch, what with a little green fluorescent makeup and bright red long fingernails," Jessica joked.

"You have a lively imagination."

"Yes, Annie. It's always been a nuisance for me," Jessica agreed vaguely.

"Annie, you're the lucky one," Sonya observed. "Barry is a friendly-seeming guy. At first sight, one could even take him for a movie heart-throb."

"Seriously, I don't really feel all that lucky," Annie confessed.

"You're being obnoxious, or else you're a wife troubled by suspicions of infidelity," Jessica surmised.

"Please, let's not be vicious. That's how rumors get started. It's just that he's been so inattentive these last few weeks; I just don't know what to think."

"Annie, you do look a little lonely. Of course, I don't mean to pry, but we are policemen's wives and must trust each other."

"Could you meet me for lunch sometime? I've got to talk to somebody about a little matter."

"Sure." Jessica smiled. "We'll set a time and place."

"Thanks." Annie smiled back. "Well, I must go find Constance. To tell her the pumpkins are now all laughing jack-o-lanterns." sexual intentions in his shorts, I know I'd

"Say, if Barry has any like to be the female on his nasty little mind," Sonya declared in an artful whisper.

"Careful. She'll hear you."

"So, I'd even give Constance something to worry about but I don't like redheaded men," She jested.

The following night, a lot of police officers came with their families to the haunted house in costumes. The lines were long on this Saturday, Halloween night. They tried to keep the crowd entertained outside on the sidewalk while they waited. A werewolf would sneak around the grown-ups to the children and sometimes hang down from an open window to sweep a furry claw in front of their faces. The admission was $5.00 for adults and .75 cents for children. All the proceeds w to go to a policeman's charity.

The doors had creaked open at 7:00 o'clock. Dressed as the villainous character, Garth Vader, of STAR WARS, Barry stood in line with Patrick and Michael Stark.

"You picked a popular costume," Brent remarked, as he took notice of several other Garth Vader's. The short, pudgy versions were extremely comical, but there were at least two other who were tall and lean, as Barry was.

"Hey Brent, do me a favor, will you?" Barry asked. "I can't lose our place in line. Take my kids inside. I've got a nature call." A laugh erupted out of both of them.

"Come on, boys!" Brent said as Count Dracula emerged waving his black cape and tucked Barry's sons under each arm like basketballs. In the torture chamber, mutated creatures came at them. The boys' screams grew louder as they went from one room to the next. Finally, from behind a wooden pillar, they watched a group of devotees, witches and warlocks, seated around a table, holding a séance, as they tried to contact the great escape artist, Harry Houdini. Just like Houdini, Barry too had disappeared for a time.

A half hour later, Brent turned sharply and fumed, "Barry, where the hell have you been? Your sons were screaming at the top of their lungs."

"That's right!" Constance rallied. "The lights all had to be turned on, so they could be escorted out of the maze."

"I'm sorry about that. I only brought Patrick and Michael after they promised me that they wouldn't work themselves up into a fit of hysteria," Barry replied in a worried tone.

"But Daddy, there was a Frankenstein's monster!"

"Both of you stop crying now," Barry urged.

"I think they're going to be just fine," Constance said in a soothing tone, and at the same time, gave Barry a coquettish glance from behind her Wonder Woman costume.

"Yes! And congratulations as chairwoman. It seems you're a howling success," Barry muttered, half under his breath.

"At any rate, too bad Annie is ill and couldn't make it," Constance added. "But wait until I talk to her-soon."

"Just as well, one Wonder Woman is more than I can handle." Exchanging thoughts, Barry grabbed his sons and walked off in search of more candy treats.

"You know, Brent, the more I see of that guy, the more I dislike him," his wife commented thoughtfully.

"Well honey bee, you did jump all over him first," Brent reminded her.

Around the block, there was a heavy police presence in the area, where the hunted and the hunter gave chase. Scrounging up the identification of the dead man, Lieutenant Bloodworth was there with a couple of lab specialists. The news reporters were taking live video as the doctor put his instruments back in his leather bag.

"How about it, Doc?"

"Lieutenant, there was nothing that could have been done. Two in the chest, one in the neck, and stomach, the truth is, he looks like a piece of Swiss cheese."

"Sure, Doc. He was knocked off in a spectacular fashion. He got a hearty welcome from his assailant."

"Pitiful too. I'd guess it was a .357 magnum."

"Don't waste your sympathy on him, Doc! He's Carlos Antonio, a noted cocaine courier out of Venezuela."

"Maybe this was a Halloween prank that was supposed to end in tragedy."

"Don't say that. All night we've had complaints about youngsters. All over the city they've been hurling eggs at cars and pedestrians. And they didn't settle on the commonplace but improvised by filling egg-shells with glue, paint and hair remover."

"Yes, that's the perfect Halloween trick," the doctor admitted. "Have you heard any more details on that crazy cop that is on the lose?"

"No, but we have appealed to anyone who can help the police unravel this baffling case. You'd be surprised to know how many people fancy themselves great detectives in this town," he added.

"Yes, I can imagine that's when all the weirdos come out of the woodwork."

"You're right and I'm tired of all of the confessions from all the cranks who are willing to confess to anything. But with any luck, we should be able to crack this case. I have as many detectives out on this one as I can spare, beating the bushes for that freak cop." He seemed rather gloomy about the prospects.

Standing in the lobby of the apartment building, a young police sergeant, Sgt. Chris Browning was tensely attentive, taking down the statements from a handful of witnesses, "You're the new doorman in the building?" he asked.

"Yes sir."

"So anyone could slip past you?"

"Yes," the doorman replied in a concise tone.

"Damn fool!" another man exclaimed.

"Sgt. Browning, I was coming back from walking my dog, Spark," an old tenant expounded, "When I spotted this man wearing a black type of costume. His face was covered. He knocked on the door of Suite 110. Then was invited in like company. A few seconds later I heard three, maybe four or five shots."

"And where were you?" another cop asked, with cynical humor.

"Me? I always use the service door." The building superintendent replied a trifle apprehensively. "I was around back in the parking lot when I saw this man in a black cape come flying down the fire escape. I thought nothing of it, just some Halloween kid."

"Lieutenant Bloodworth, some potential witnesses have begged that they not be forced to testify when we make the capture," Sgt. Browning reported, holding his clipboard to his chest.

"What do you want me to do? I'm satisfied the citizens of the city of New York are permeated by fear," he acknowledged.

In something of an irksome tone, the Doctor remarked, "Bloodworth, what is the use, when you have some witnesses who will knowingly and willfully commit perjury rather than testify against a known criminal?"

"Hell, even so more dramatic are the witnesses who are frightened to a point where they prefer to go to jail rather than testify," the lieutenant said, standing outside in the soft, sweet air of night.

On the sidewalk, four tenants, including a white-haired old lady, were assembled in a group, watching them take the body of the murder victim away.

"Like I said, Doc., these building tenants are surprisingly normal." Their eyes locked as their cheeks puffed out with suppressed laughter.

THE DOMESTIC SITUATION
CHAPTER 10

BUMMED, BARRY WRESTLES with the thought of how he might best explain his domestic situation to JeZe Bella, but she learns of it on her own, and sees in this a truly legitimate reason for terminating her relationship with him. It was early dawn. The sun's rays were striking the tall buildings. When the cell phone rang, JeZe Bella woke up, surprised. Suppressing a little yawn, she put her fingers to her now faded lips, and sat back down on the edge of her bed. She obviously did not want to speak with anyone as the cell phone chimed madly on the nightstand.

"JeZe Bella," Barry said, when at last she lifted the receiver, "I called to see how you were. And have you missed me a little?"

"If you want to know, nothing has changed," she retorted and shook her head vehemently.

"Why the hell not?" Frustrated, Barry banged his hand against the car window as the early morning sunlight started to shine directly into his eyes.

"Barry, you haven't been listening to what I'm saying. I really don't need this problem at my doorstep. You're still a married man and that's not my game."

"JeZe Bella, don't lay a guilt trip on me. Annie and I once talked about divorce, but she insisted that if we were to divorce, she would take the boys, you know-full custody. And on top of child support, she wanted a real bundle of alimony."

"I'd figured she'd do what she thought was best for her and your kids."

"True, and if I disagreed, she'd listen politely to my reason, and then go ahead with her own plans to get even."

"And suppose she'll ask you for more than fifty-five hundred a month?"

"You know my financial situation."

"And you know mine. I won't be the other woman." At that, she tried to cut the conversation short.

"JeZe Bella, I'd like some understanding from you. My marriage is a disastrous one. The relationship is sterile, and has been for some time now."

"Barry. What you get out of life depends, for the most part, on what you put into it," she remarked, cradling the cell phone on her right shoulder.

"JeZe Bella, you're upset. I just don't want to see you because you're pretty. Or because I'm horny for you, I only want to talk to you, hoping you'll change your mind."

"For the good of whom, may I ask?"

"For our good," he insisted with emphasis. "If you can call it good."

"And what if I can't?"

"Who are you kidding now, JeZe Bella?"

"Boy, you've got me all wrong. I'm not about to break up your marriage or anyone else's, for that matter. I'm just not made that way."

"What about us? I thought-"

"Never!"

"Now I'm upset. Listen, why we don't discuss this carefully over dinner somewhere tonight. Please don't let me beg you.

"Barry," she hedged, "that's impossible. I thought I'd bake bread. tonight."

"What is this, a new-found interest in home economics?"

"Look, I don't like your catty remarks."

"All right, but you just be at the Hilton at 7:30 tonight." His dictatorial tone gave her a sudden chill; the words were like a threat. As she placed the cell phone back on the nightstand, she wondered if she dared risk the consequences of a no-show.

Thinking quickly, Barry is not so easily dissuaded, insisting that he and Annie have often talked of divorce and promises that a legal separation is now inevitable. They say the Devil is a roaring Lion but since he does not appear to have any concrete plan in mind, JeZe Bella adamantly refuses to see him again. Ditto! What follows is a difficult period for Barry, whose relationships at home remain strained, and who vents his frustrations by becoming more aggressive in his role as a Police Officer. Looking down at a newspaper it was about all the partisan politics and bickering at the police precinct. He would not be a wet blanket but the voice of reason that JeZe Bella must understand as he remembered her saying, "There has to be another time and place for us. We are to close as a wet kiss and further than miles apart in all our thoughts and yet a step away from each other's' arms.' Standing there he knew he couldn't outrun his deepest fear or the monster in himself and could not escape her innocent wish. But going on his gut he focused all attention to the street as he stammered and sputtered. His tight-lips sneering back over his white teeth filled with menace as she was not his target. Feeling an infant's slumber, he thought of his precinct Captain Tanner. Grilling all his men in blue about crime statistics and any and all questionable shootings by officers of the department. Captain Tanner always soared over them like a hawk descending. As Barry Stark floated with casual ease under his radar. Working the streets like a bulldog well beyond the borders of the Metro Precinct. But in all the pissing and moaning that got pretty detailed, Barry was a smart cop. With an extra tick on everybody that crossed his sight. He was very polite to a point and a wink, and all his cop bodies knew it. In the riveting drama and stunning crimes rooted in total revenge and social injustice the hard way. He was the nemeses of pure evil that collided with a beauty among the highest towers of NYC, the island of man.

STYMIED AND ON THE CARPET
CHAPTER 11

UPTOWN AT THE main precinct, with murders in the city police Meanwhile, had stop the feuding among his men. "I know you've questioned several dozen officers this morning," he said. "Any promising leads now that the Halloween Murder of Carlos Antonio is tied into the Crusader for justice, and Black Lives Matters foundation?"

"Abraham, I have no choice," the Lieutenant retorted, "But to cover all the ground I can."

Stifling a yawn, the police Chief said, "It is all too astounding." "So tell me about this Barry Stark, National Reserve and Marine Vet. He enjoys the rough stuff and was a block away when this killing took place," the Lieutenant said impatiently.

"So were a couple dozen other police officers. There are witnesses to that. Don't forget we live in tyranny. Sure, Barry Stark has nearly killed two or three criminals in the line of duty. But then, this is New York."The chief thumbed through a stack of personnel records in his file cabinet as he spoke.

"Obviously, this cop Stark has a violent temper."

"Lieutenant, who has complained about his drunkenness?" the chief managed to keep a straight face.

"Some of his beer buddies, from the Bronx."

"Pay no attention to that. They're all brawlers at heart. Besides, I don't think we've exhausted the possibility of all the men on the force."

The Lieutenant mulled that question over for a while and made a mental list of everyone under suspicion.

"No, Chief, but Stark is by far my favorite candidate. Somehow, I will get a handle on him."

"He's still a pretty small fish, come to think of it."

"No, all I know is that this Stark has a generous life insurance policy on his wife and his sons would get the bulk of it."

"I don't know why you keep harping on that particular cop. If there is something incriminating here, well find it."The chief sighed. "And I was planning on going to Cape Cod for the weekend, a fanciful idea."

They looked at one another a bit uncertainly, and then laughed. "Just let me say that one of these days, Stark will go too far with his pleasure and wind-up doing time," the Lieutenant predicted somberly.

"Look, I know the cop is cocky and brash at times. You can't prosecute on suspicion alone."

"No Chief, but we all louse up at some time. Then I'll be waiting." "The law will take care of him. And whoever else, for that matter."

"Abraham, what is it? An eye for an eye, to point out last week's the sidewalk killing of a cop in Manhattan. And then a shootout a day later that brought down his alleged attacker."

"I am concerned about the recent wave of crime, with some of the Black and Hispanic kids in the streets looting indiscriminately. The shop owners keep shouting 'Kill them, kill them all.' It's the same questions and answers. 'Why, do you do this looting, son?' 'In order to live, I have to steal.' 'What do the police want? Stop the crime, keep the peace, catch the criminal and enforce the law."

"I can't forget the public consciousness has snapped, arguing that cops by nature are too trigger-happy accept when they need protection."

"Lieutenant, I'm not blind to our policeman's faults," the chief said. "Yes, I was hired to do a job but I also have to look out for the other guys on our team."

"Well, deadly force is not the only answer, Chief."

"You sound like Huck from Internal Affairs. I refuse to constrain any of my men in the use of their fire arm's power."

"I don't mean to upset you, Chief. We have been friends for a long time now. I really think you're being derelict in your duties. The city police force must weed out this undesirable element, ASAP."

"Hell now, you sound like the mayor. He's got this campaign on changing the image of the street's cycle cops on the force. Uptown, he is mounting a recruiting drive." The Chief amended. "He wants the Ivy League type fresh out of college with no military background for the asphalt jungle we are living in."

"We all have our part to do the pressure is defiantly on."

"Yes, and it's going to be difficult, but I've got to gain control of my own men or suffer the consequences."

"Then there are boundary lines that further confuse the issue."

"No," he said, putting his head down.

Stymied by his record, Barry Stark is called on the carpet for this, and his personality profile is reviewed, revealing a number of physical encounters. With various suspects, and is thought to be wavering on the brink of some crisis point. A sore question it is generally believed that, he should be more closely supervised and that his behavior should be carefully monitored for the first signs of unreasonable, even erratic behavior or a lapse in judgment.

It was 3:30 p.m. in the warm afternoon. The sun was beating down hard on the sweltering asphalt that looked as if it were wet from the reflecting heat. On this hot, sticky day the sound of two high-power motorcycles grew loud and clamorous, and then stopped abruptly in the middle of a rundown tenement block, emptying the street of their noise.

"Buddy, would you look at that! A slob of a old woman."

"Big, isn't she?" Brent had begun to run his fingers around his collar. It was a relief to laugh at something or someone. Barry threw a hand across Brent's shoulders. "Yes, she has the big brown bolting eye of a stupid cow."

"Barry, I could go for a cold beer and a big slice of Vanzetti's Pizza. How about you?"

"Sure, but we have an hour to go yet," Barry reminded him, and wiped the sweat from his brow.

"Barry, what do you make of Lieutenant Bloodworth?"

"There are several answers I could give you besides thorough and persistent. Like an old fart."

"Yeah, I'd like nothing better than to piss on his face," Brent admitted. "He just put me through the wringer before noon. He had it in his mind that I might be the cop they're looking for."

"Look Pal, they're going after everybody. He's looking for a sacrificial lamb. You should have heard him with me earlier," Barry said with dramatic emphasis. "He's fishing for a bite."

"You mean he accused you of murder?"

"Not in so many words. The implication was there but I told the guy I was a damned Christian. And he didn't go for it. I'm still on his shit-list of number one suspects."

"Barry, I can't help but feel that I'm leading the list."

"I can't believe that. You just don't have the stomach for that sort of thing. Brent, I went to lunch with three other buddies. We compared notes on the Lieutenant's interrogations. I was careful enough to refer to him as the little lieutenant, as the guys cracked jokes about me being that cop."

Brent frowned at the mild levity. "Does he think we're so emotionally tied up in our work that we'd kill street garbage?"

"Lord, I bet if he went to a hockey game and heard me shout, 'Kill the goalie', he'd have me arrested on the spot," Barry joked, working sports into the conversation.

"I guess we're all caught in this unholy tide."

"Hey, are you going to let that asshole call you a killer?" Barry asked and menaced him with his weapon. Hearing a harmless click, his finger covered the trigger and the safety was off.

Red-face, Brent laughed again. He seemed to be enjoying the situation. "Somebody shot the creep with a .32-caliber pistol, real morbid."

"Brent, did you see it happen?"

"No, man, but you were gone a half hour that night."

"Well, will you please shut up before I get blamed for it?"

"Don't get mad. The Lieutenant likes to bust my fruity ass too."

"Let's split." Barry wasn't playing the game which was quite a feat. That encompasses his life from the beginning to an end. With such documentary like precision, that it seemed credible. He had ever existed in all the unhappiness life had given him. Barry had urged Brent again to leave the matter alone and was quite vehement that only increased Brent's suspicions. But Barry reminded him of their profession and had suggested this kind of gossip could propagate and be embellished out of proportion. Barry knew he had some power and influence over Brent. Even though Brent felt stuck in the middle over a shameful petty of a joke. He compromises by the politics and apologized for the presumption and his impulsiveness.

Luckily Barry was gracious and had said, "As far as I'm concerned the matter is closed buddy."

Brent felt he did not trust his own instincts and presupposed malice toward his best friend Barry. He now had experienced a form of grief, intense and very pure - then laughed and may have sounded stupidly, "Barry, please don't listen to my babble."

"If only it were as easy as all that Brent!" Barry flipped him off as a joke.

They now parted ways and Brent flashed him a thumbs-up of approval. Their motorcycles kick on as the two men spun off in different directions.

Passing by the garment district, Brent had to stop to pick up the New York Times on his way home. There wasn't much new on the Halloween murder. Brent knew some of the guys would be considered a traitor giving in. Yet, there were lots of other suspicious cops, not overly. Why, Barry? He thought. Possibly because of his icy manner and those trigger eyes. But like a quirk, there was a moment that stuck in his mind and then faded. "Hell, some reporter will probably dig up the truth and make it look like an old Watergate cover-up."

Later that evening, feeling strung-out, Barry collapsed on the couch, trying to sort out the whole day in his confused mind. But with half-closed eyes, he watched Annie descend the hall stairs and sneak up beside him.

"Tickle, tickle," she mused, pressing her fingers to his firm rib cage.

Annie, I'm too tired. Please don't pester me with your childish game," he said in a drowsy condescending voice.

"Sure thing dear, you don't have to draw me a picture."

"Do you really want to go there?" he asked then, grasping her around the throat, but very gently. "Sometimes I'd like to strangle you, woman."

"Ahh," she sighed, "But then you'd never know about the little bit of good news I have to tell you." She said to his inappropriate remark.

"Get to the point. I have no idea what you're talking about. Or is this just another of your foolish games?"

"Barry, you're so mentally and sexually abusive. What do you want, oral sex? How can I talk to you in this manner?"

He had slipped the large palm of his hand under her blouse in order to take hold of her round, soft breast. But gently, she pushed his hand away. Kissing her, his lips moved over hers and his tongue searched in her mouth. Annie turned, pushing him away again, as he tried to loosen his belt a notch. Barry soon realized she had no desire to be aroused. She had this mental picture of him as a rasping, argumentative cop, having shouted in order to draw attention to him.

"If you'll excuse me, dear, I can see about your dinner."

Climaxing the scene, Patrick and Michael raced in through the kitchen door, greeting their father effusively with a wild warble of screams. They soon knocked him off balance and wrestled him on to the floor. Simultaneously, Annie grabbed the gun away from Barry's hand for safety's sake, as he struggled to pull free from the boys, hopelessly weakened by playful laughter and boyish slang.

Throughout this period, Barry remains preoccupied with the thought of affecting some reconciliation with JeZe Bella. At what dream state had his fascination with her become an obsession? Life with a twist, he is tormented! The thought, that someone else might stare at her as hotly as he could. As expectantly that someone else, someone soon, will know the intense rapture, the insatiable demands she is capable of expressing. He begins to develop a twisted concept of her relationship with and affection for, a young professional photographer whom JeZe Bella openly credits with making her a top Model.

The perfect antidote, "The path to hell is paved with hot coals.' As for Barry, he was in a fretful state of confusion filled with despair in every aspect of life. Still bitter and smug he will carry on the affair with a trace of will power.

THE INSANITY COMES
CHAPTER 12

LOSING SLEEP, THE name of Tony Savage is a constant sound in his head, a constant reminder that a closer, more intimate relationship between the two of them must be averted at all costs. Barry implores her to meet with him, endures her haughty, sarcastic, painful refusals, and persists in a kind of desperate heat that ultimately wears her down. In the paranoid craziness, JeZe Bella agrees to meet him in a out-of-the-way hotel restaurant. While in another part of town, Annie Stark has arranged a luncheon date of her own. To a close personal friend, Annie confesses that she is pregnant, and expresses her fears that Barry will feel trapped by the news in view of his edgy infrequent attentions toward her. It was the middle of the day. Jessica was waiting for Annie in a coffee shop, right across the street from the sleazy Savoy Hotel and bar.

"I'm sorry I'm late, but the babysitter almost didn't show-up."

They sat by the window, taking in the afternoon sunlight.

"I'm no marriage counselor after the fact," Jessica disclosed. "I wish I had never split up with my first husband but I was so young and he no wiser." She sounds convincing in reminiscent.

The service was slow; twenty minutes later their order was taken by a gum-chewing gangly waitress. They resisted looking from the window as some cops hurried an angry gentleman out of the Savoy bar into the back seat of a patrol car and sped away with no attention drawn in the broad day-light.

"Jessica, I must swear you to secrecy," Annie pleaded, placing her cup down. "You must promise.

"I'm listening."

"You're not to discuss this with anyone. A few weeks ago, I found out I was pregnant, and now the other day, my GOB confirmed it."

"Annie, that's wonderful!"

"No, you don't understand. This will only make Barry feel more tied down to me. It's a threat to his very nature."

"Then don't worry, Annie. You can have an abortion done at Plan Parenthood in one day. No one would have to know, not even Barry. I know, because I had one done six months ago."

"Jessica, I'm Catholic. It's against everything I believe in, and everything I was ever taught."

"Then, as hopeless as it may seem, my poor Annie, you will have to tell your husband."

Annie lightened up, distraught, then a smile broke through and she slowly nodded her head.

"Annie, don't cry! This could be exactly what's needed to bring the two of you closer than ever," The friend remarked with a perennial optimism. It was something that Annie would also like to believe, but no longer does. The friend vows to keep her condition a secret until she can decide upon the best way to approach Barry.

Slowly, the sun set over the city with great brilliancy on the orange autumn- colored trees. Soon the chalk-white moon took over, casting its luminous brightness upon the dark pavement. On this chilly November in front of the ritzy Hilton Hotel, without the benefit of hype, Barry Stark appeared at the stroke of eight O'clock. He had come casually dressed in a pair of brand-new blue jeans, a flannel shirt, black Stetson and an English tweed sport jacket.

It was clear from the outset that JeZe Bella did not feel very well. But it took a moment to determine exactly why. "You're late," she observed curiously. "You did say 7:30?" she asked, outfitted in western duds, like an urban cowgirl, with a fur vest and a string of rhinestones at her waist and hips.

"JeZe Bella, I couldn't get away any sooner."

"I take it you're under suspicion. Well, if I were her, I'd tell you to blow."

"You like to aggravate me, don't you?' he said, and doubled up his fists in a threatening gesture.

"If that's what you think, why don't you just let me leave and spare us both a lot of unpleasantness?"

"Never mind, I just lost my head. I'm sorry. It's just that I've been so anxious to see you. It made me mad as hell to get held up."

"So you say."

"It's true. C'mon now, whataya say?"

"Nothing doing, I've listened to your obscene mouth before."

"Look," he said, drawing him up in another of his threatening gestures, "If you're tempted to stand here and express opinions----well, don't." He clamored.

"You're right, of course,"JeZe Bella conceded. "This sort of thing doesn't help either of us. But I can't promise you anything at this point." Having to say these words gave her a funny feeling in the pit of her stomach.

"Obviously, you think I'm a bastard."

She shook her head vigorously. "That isn't what I think at all, that's what you think."

"Really?"

"Of course, and what's more you know it."

He stood looking at her speculatively for a moment. "Let's go inside," he suggested finally, having managed to get his complex under control. The parking attendant was staring at them rudely. They pretended not to notice.

She smiled at him, but he couldn't be sure what was running through her mind as the sparkle of her dark eyes caught his.

Inside the hotel restaurant, the setting looked like a cocktail party on a garden terrace. The sound of voices and the clinking of glasses could be heard throughout the large outdoor supper room with strings of hanging white lights.

After a few moments, Barry noticed JeZe Bella picking at her Caesar salad. "You're eating in a bloody hurry," he observed then, a trifle unhappy.

"Yes, I'm terribly sorry about that. But I've got an early morning photo session and can't afford dark circles under my eyes for lack of sleep."

"What are you saying?"

"That we'll have to cut this evening short, I do have a job."

Barry stared blankly at her for a moment, and then said, "That all sounds like an alibi to me." He smirked.

"And you sound like a prosecuting attorney," JeZe Bella retorted, in a playful attempt to lighten his mood.

Barry's plate was filled, heaped high with hot roast beef, a baked potato, beans and salad. For a while they ate with the intimacy of lovers, neither of them wanting to mention the subject of divorce, although it dominated the evening even so. As she leaned toward him, she caught the scent of his aromatic Copenhagen after-shave cologne. Exhaling deeply through her glossy red lips, prolonging the moment, they talked of little things. Then JeZe Bella took another small sip of her wine and stared at him. He was certainly different from what she had expected a cop in regular clothes to be like and whom blended in as any male model would in the opulent country décor.

"Cheers!" he said, as he lifted his wine glass and proposed a toast. JeZe Bella's eyes grew wide, and as their glasses touched, she began to tell him a little more about her.

"I'm only twenty-two years old, Barry. I came to New York two years ago, as soon as I had saved up enough money to get here. It's funny, but you want to hear something? My Mother still thinks I should come back home and Marry Marco Vargas, the boy next door. He is the high school jock type and will graduate from junior college this spring semester."JeZe Bella reached under the table for his hand. Barry resisted looking at her but she didn't need him to look upon her with approval. Even though she had made up this lie about her checkered pass.

"Barry, what is your wife like?" JeZe Bella asked then.

Instead of answering her question, she watched his eyes narrow in an angry or suspicious way, but didn't know the reason until a tall older man suddenly approached them.

"JeZe Bella! I recognized you at once!" the man beamed, and bent over her hand, kissing it with a kind of old continental flair.

"You have an extraordinary memory----Roger," JeZe Bella replied, somewhat embarrassed and nervous.

"Why, two years isn't such a long time," her mysterious admirer replied, and stroked a perfect goatee, ignoring Barry entirely. "Well, lovely angel, I'll be on my way, see you soon."

Avoiding Barry's steady gaze, JeZe Bella looked down into her lap and said, "Well now, I certainly didn't expect to run into him here, or anywhere. You meet many people in this business, and then all of us go our separate ways. Why, I just barely managed to remember his name. He's a major buyer for a chain of department stores over on the west coast-Macy's, I think. He bought everything I modeled on my first job and was it a break for the agency I was working for."

"Maître' check please." With a kind of aggressive flamboyance Barry dropped a hundred dollar on the table and grabbed her abruptly by the arm. As JeZe Bella lurched to her feet, she tossed her shoulder bag over her arm. They walked out of the restaurant in silence, both victims of their inner tension and conflict over this male buyer.

"Slow down, Barry, before I lose my boot heels," she exclaimed.

Angrily, Barry refuses to believe her. Banging his big fist on the door, he hurls a round of heated accusations and insults at her. The sound of his voice burned through her like hot coals and as she struggled for a dignified reply, all words failed her, and then, in a rash impulsive move, she ran from him and hailed a cab as it slowly turned the corner.

"Step on it, driver, before that yo-yo catches up with me!" she said, and slammed the cab-door with an oddly determined air.

"JeZe Bella, wait up! Barry's voice called out in the background. "JeZe Bella, come back!"

But it was too late, for in the twinkling of an eye, she had left him behind in the cool neon night. Meanwhile, Barry's meeting with her was alternately pleasant and then volatile. As JeZe Bella had revealed a little more of herself, explaining the ambitious manner in which she had gone through in order to escape the small-island life she had always despised and the lie she told him. Barry is amazed at this sudden intensity of feeling, the big uneasy. He is confident that whatever must be accomplished or overcome in order for he and JeZe Bella to be together is a price that must be paid willingly, and with no regrets, knowing the outer reserve and formality of his true nature. Like in a hall of mirrors, glancing at his reflection in the hotel restaurant window his facial features shine as he struts to his car with a puffed chest and muscled arms, realizing he is too totally in love as in a trance, he could smell and position himself behind her; wrapping his arms around her small waist, tight like a squished bug on a windshield.

Suffering from a case of insomnia, Annie sat in bed reading. She knew she couldn't beat Satan at his own game. The shadowy night provided the perfect backdrop. Then silently she heard the sound of Barry's heavily boot-clad step coming up the stairs. A half hour later, Barry sat on the toilet seat in side their white porcelain bathroom, staring at the electric bulb.

"Did you see her tonight?" Annie asked loudly.

"See, who?" he replied, stirring out of his silence.

It had been a long time since she had talked to him as directly as this.

"You're sickening, if you ask me," Annie said crossly.

"I stand accused, but what about the other night? When you had cramps and I fell asleep waiting." His voice echoed over the flush of the toilet bowl. "There is nothing for me but to take it to the street. I've had it with your Christianity." He said indignantly.

Betrayed, her eyes were bright with tears as she caught herself blinking them back irritably.

"So, what do you feel for me now-contempt?" he asked drily.

"No, I have never felt that," she said, slamming her bible shut.

"You're a faithless husband and there is nothing much I can do about it right now."

"Nothing, short of fatal!" He remained unmoved. She felt her knees knocking as he pushed her senselessly aside and climbed into their king bed.

Annie virtually fell on her hands and knees, crying. She sensed something was wrong. She knew another woman had entered his life and suspected he had been out with her tonight. But Barry acted totally oblivious to her cries and pleas. He lay stretched out on the bed, scratching through his white briefs. Immediately, he felt smitten by the thought of JeZe Bella, in this romantic tug-ofwar between her sensuous charms and this heatedly ironic marriage problem. With brooding charisma, Barry's alpha male gaze dogged Annie. He was tired of sparring over her cliched dialogue in their claustrophobic bedroom. All he wanted now was a little peace and some sleep escape.

CLOUDLESS AND COLD
CHAPTER 13

ENJOYING THE MOMENT Barry and Brent straddled on to their motorcycles, ridding them into heavy noon traffic. This fall day was cloudless and cold on Second Avenue. Inside the restaurant, Avanti, the people spoke a mixture of Italian and English. Seated at a red checker table that easily accommodated their group of six, Tony Savage said, "When in Rome, do as the Romans do. In other words, ladies, you may pig out."

Frank Sinatra and old-world music added a certain charm to the place. There was the sweet smell of antipasto in the air. Seated in this quaint dining-room, JeZe Bell was heard to remark, "Since you were all good enough to treat me to lunch, I will try the Scampi and Veal Parmesan." She made a kind of announcement of her order, twirling the red napkin between her fingers.

"Delicioso appetite," the swarthy Italian waiter replied warmly.

"What is Calamari?" Maria Torres muttered softly.

"Oh, squid but stick to the basics," another girl said. "Lasagna or spaghetti with meatballs should do the trick."

"No, if I'd wanted to play it safe, I'd have gone to the Pizza Palace."

"Will somebody ask the waiter to enlighten us on this menu before I die of hunger?" Ronnie Love injected above the amber glow of the candle on their table.

While the mysteries of this fine Southern Italian cuisine were under

Discussion, Tony reviewed the wine list of burgundy and imported roses.

"Waiter, I will have the scungilli and pasta. Oh, and two bottles of Chianti," he said, as if it were the most natural thing in the world.

Suddenly, the slinky models looked at one another, a bit uncertain amid their giggles and their parody.

"Tony, please! We can't go back to a photo session all tipsy." JeZe Bella objected.

"Ahh now, where's your sense of daring, my girl? At any rate, today's your birthday, and that gives us every reason to make an exception. How old are you, by the way? Twenty-three, isn't it?" he joked knowing full well.

As the girls sang Happy Birthday to her, JeZe Bella concealed her flushed face behind the red napkin.

As they all reminisced about their own careers at agency, the time swiftly passed.

"How about dessert now, cake?" Tony urged, and once again signaled for their jolly waiter.

"Heavens no, Tony, they all cried in unison, even as a familiar handsome face emerges in the entrance. Confident and in full control, Barry Stark stood hovering over their private table, accompanied by his partner, Officer Brent Barrett. Tall and tan Barry towered over her table, looking dapper in his navy-blue uniform. He resisted the urge to apologize for the interruption. His smile revealed prefect white teeth and realized he should not speak and forever hold the peace with her.

"I thought it was you, Barry," JeZe Bella said. "I recognized your shadow standing in the doorway."

As she made the introductions, Barry nodded his head curtly and mustered up a handshake. That was firm and almost painful to her flaxen blond photographer Tony Savage. She tried hard to sound enthusiastic after seeing him again with so many hurtful feelings still inside her. to everyone present and began to unzip his warm leather jacket. Meanwhile, the inhibited eyes of the models danced across Barry's body and tightly drawn crotch, appraising him as if he were a prize bull at a rodeo.

"I'll bet you get hustled all the time," one of the girls remarked with a low whistle.

Turning away from her steamy glare, Barry acknowledged the greeting of the waiter.

"Officer Stark. Long time no sees! How may we help you?" "I just stopped in for some coffee and a plate of hot Fettuccini, Claudio. My partner Brent would like the same."

He was straight forward and gripping. He had carried over them like thunder, potentially dangerous. Then tautly he turned away, with helmet in hand, and the daily newspaper tucked under his arm. Marching off, the two officers seemed to flaunt the law in some adolescent way. With their male grinding walk and hard outward leer, they had a crushing impact upon JeZe Bella, who rose to her feet, feeling weak and numb.

"Excuse me for a moment," she said to the group. "I just remembered that I have a book to pick up at the Barns & Noble store around the corner. They special-ordered it for me, I need it to finish this needlepoint project I started."

Maria wanted to snicker over the situation but managed to hold her breath.

"Sure, JeZe," Tony interceded diplomatically. "We'll see you back at my van."

"Hah! Those two don't fool me for a moment," Maria snorted.

"It's ridiculous. JeZe, ought to know better," Ronnie said with a grimace.

"Oh, I don't know," Tony responded casually, and slid a fifty-dollar tip under one of the saucers. After pooling their funds, they waited as Tony went to pay the young cashier, noticing that he took the time to steal a look over his shoulder at Barry and Brent who were seated at the coffee counter. As Barry sat on one of the red tools with perfect posture and shoulders back to their table. He gazed up at himself in the wide mirror over the long lunch counter top. While today's midtown traffic was at an absolute standstill, he felt livid in the heat of things. There was more to all this beneath the surface and the models relentless idle chatter behind them.

Unfolding his newspaper, Barry observed, "You know, buddy, I didn't even know it was JeZe Bella's birthday."

Avoiding the subject entirely, Brent replied, "Barry, there's a memo out concerning the spring picnic. Are you going to sign up for the golf tournament?"

"Well, it was fun last year, playing against the other precincts. In any case, my box is always stuffed with memos. This one probably got transferred to the wastebasket."

"Still, it might not hurt to get in a few practice shots." Brent mused. "What with the tournament still a few months away, we'd have enough time to really shape up."

"More coffee officers, I have a fresh pot?"

"No thanks, Rosa." Barry said, turning his attention back to Brent, he added, "Not a bad idea. I haven't even looked at a putter in months."

"By the way, Barry, I'll be wearing loud yellow threads how about you."

"Sure! I was thinking my old light blue or burgundy. You know, I'd really like to get JeZe Bella something today. Come with me to a store?"

"I can't. And you shouldn't either. The Chief doesn't like us taking time off the job."

"Don't talk to me about that hog headed bastard. In case you didn't know it, I just hate fat people."

Walking out into the fresh air with a pair of lovely models on each arm, Tony glanced back at the busy Italian restaurant a trifle ruefully.

"I hope JeZe doesn't ever run into him again." He added.

"I guess it's my fault for suggesting this place," Julie Larrabee said. "But my Italian boyfriend and I often come here and it seemed like a nice change."

"You couldn't have known what would happen,"Tony responded matter-of-factly. "The fact is, we're in his turf. As far as that goes, I'm sure JeZe knows that."

"Okay, I just don't want to be the blame for any of this.

" No way could you be. Come on, let's go."

"Tony's right, Julie. It is really a very nice place to have lunch."

"Even so, I feel as if everything was spoiled," Julie countered, a trifle petulantly.

"Well, it wasn't. We all had a grand time. And the food was terrific."

"Good," Julie said with a long sigh. "I'll be sure to compliment the chef the next time I'm in."

Later in the afternoon, Barry went on an errand to select something as a birthday gift for JeZe Bella. He went in hope that this gesture would somehow mend things between them. Oddly enough, he stopped in front of The Gilded Cage, a pet store on the side street. He stared into the large display window. Inside were marvelous birds of every size and species, sitting in cages or atop perches, pecking at seeds and warbling their songs. The exotic birds ranged from macaws to cockatiels, and there were also parrots, parakeets, finches and lovebirds.

As soon as Barry walked into the shop, the birds began to behave in a hysterical manner. It was as if some animalistic sense warned them of impending danger as they beat their wings against the bars of their enclosures.

"What the hell is happening?" the shop owner yelled, amid a profusion of flying feather. He could not think of what to do with all these birds squawking in deadly terror.

"Officer, please, you'll have to leave! You're upsetting my birds!" the shopkeeper insisted.

Having to leave abruptly, Barry found that he was trembling and that he had broken into a feverish sweat. Flashes of fluorescent orange blazed across his searing eyes. Reeling slightly, he steadied himself against the wall of the building. His mind was blank and his face felt numb. After a moment, he put his helmet back on. Growling angrily under his breath at the thought of the reception he had just received, he clenched his fists tightly as if all the fiends of hell had won. Then he wedged forward on the motorcycle that let out a thundering roar down the street.

FLOWERS FOR MY LADY
CHAPTER 14

THE NEXT MORNING, waking from a dreamlike state, JeZe Bella wrenched her mascaraed eyes open. With sweaty palms and a heart beating wildly over a series of thoughts, images and emotions that occurred during her sound sleep, she stood before the full length brass mirror, examining her beautiful face. Searching for something in her own reflection, there came to mind the painful past that still continued to haunt her and the lie she told to Barry.

The day had gone by less than a snail's pace. It was now Saturday afternoon. Clamping a sheet of drawing paper to her easel, JeZe Bella began to draw with feverish strokes. Having drawn a self portrait, she now tried to cloud over an expression she had captured. But it was no use. The anger in her tortured eyes knew the truth. As if driven by some other, uglier instinct, she tore into the paper grudgingly, the hurt she felt rippled like the shimmering surface of the ocean. Unexpectedly, there came a too familiar knock on the door. She quickly moved to cover the self-portrait and went to answer the door with frivolous anticipation.

"Why Barry, thank you! The big birthday bouquet is just lovely," she said, and pulled him inside quite easily for he offered no resistance.

"JeZe Bella, I can't stay," he told her uneasily. "I'm supposed to be on my way to the neighborhood bar, Harley's, to play some pool with my buddy, Brent and some of the guys on the police force."

"All the same, you must give me time to thank you properly. The flowers came late last night-all twenty-three red long-stemmed roses. Tell you what, why don't you pretend that your friends have found a replacement for you at Harley's?" her eyes shone with the first glimmer of an intimidating notion.

"Well, and what's brought about this new change?" he wanted to know, with a defanged smile.

Her mouth formed a small "Oh" as she moved forward with two crystal wine glasses and offered him a taste of dark Chablis.

At last, they were reunited in a tantalizing moment of warm sex, and as JeZe Bella clung to him, and caught the fresh scent of his spicy breath, she knew it was enough that he was back in her canopy bed, and that there was no longer any need for forgiveness. As the night would fall through the open curtains, Barry turned over with glazed eyes and asked what time it was.

"Only a little after nine," she told him.

"I've got to go, where is my underwear?"

"You weren't wearing any but be reasonable, Barry. It's not that late." She watched him shake his head as if to clear it, and then he rose from her silky pink bed sheets.

"I've missed dinner," he said. Taking note of two empty wine bottles lying on the floor, he could see what had happened. "I might as well be delirious, the condition I'm in."

"Surely you're not ready to throw this night away."

"Don't start, please. I ought to skin you alive. Where's my sweater?" he asked, fighting the urge of his churning stomach. "So, that's it, huh? After that big manly display, you put on at Avanti's?"

"Look, there's something you'd better get through your silly head," he said in a no-nonsense tone. "I can't do what I want no matter how important I am to myself."

"Meaning what?"

"Meaning, that you should see, there are three people in my life. Who mean a lot to me, you JeZe Bella, and my two sons?"

"Well, if I mean so much, when will I see you again?"

"I don't know exactly. Thanksgiving is right around the corner. That's another family holiday."

"I see. Well, then maybe we'd better finish it here and now. I can see I'll never be any more than just a blatant affair."

"Do you think I'm stupid? That I can't see that you're trying to force the issue? Well, it won't work. There are too many problems involved, too many things beneath the surface."

"Then let me make it easy for you. I'll remove one problem by removing myself. This is good-bye, Barry. When you leave today, that will be it for us." She watched him slipping on his shoes and move silently toward the door in tight fitted Levi's that rode up his butt. It did not seem possible that he could go without a parting word, and yet he did. Thinking her heart had stalled, did she sacrifice her love and sex even if it was somewhat dysfunctional? She had ended an affair that turned out to be more than just physical. JeZe Bella, still felt his warm lips on her's, tracing her finger on her red lips. She had her own best interest at heart even as his painted picture had tarnished in her mind. "Barry Stark! You've taken my heart and crush it under your feet." His sexiness left her feeling a bit smutty. But one bad look from him made her die on the vine. It was all about alpha dominance with him. At that moment she couldn't understand how he could look so swoony and be such a motherfucker at best as she fell back into her bed crying.

TRAPPED AND CORNERED
CHAPTER 15

BARRY'S THOUGHTS ARE capable of feeling many things in life. What was so commonly familiar or rare and extraordinary, with the fireplace burning, the air thin and dry, it was like a bad joke, trapped and cornered. Over the family-oriented holiday of thanksgiving, the Stark's make an earnest effort to present a united front to Annie's parents, who come to enjoy some time with their grandchildren. For the most part, it was a pleasant day, Annie's parents, the Morgan's, had driven down from Boston to have dinner with Annie, Barry and the boys. Outside the dining room picture window, the breeze ruffled through the autumn leaves of tall trees. On this special occasion, Barry was smiling. There was something in his eyes that made him seem happy. Surrounded by family, he held out his arms and Annie swept into them, holding a large platter.

"What do we have here? The whole nine yards, and my favorite fixings!" his voice boomed into every corner of the room.

"Yes, dear, a tender roast turkey with some old-fashioned dressing."

"Let me help you, Annie." He kissed her tenderly on the cheek and took the platter from her.

"How delicious it all looks!" Mr. Morgan said and settled back into his chair.

"Please don't forget---I helped chop, peel, and stuff, even baste that old bird," Mrs. Morgan said over the murmurs of approval that came from her grandsons at the sight of the golden-brown turkey.

After the family had bowed their heads in prayer, they attacked the meal with great gusto, although little turkey was eaten by the boys. They continued to eye the pumpkin pie as if it were in danger of disappearing.

Barry chuckled softly and said, "You boys can't wait, eh? Well, I can't think of anyone who could criticize you for that."

A puzzled look crossed Annie's face like a delicate cloud. Half under her breath, she said, "Barry, I think you've let my Dad have too much wine."

"I suppose you're right," he responded lightheartedly, "But then, this is a holiday, isn't it? Why don't you cut the boys a big slice of pie and pile a lot of whipped cream on top?"

"No dear because, they haven't finished all their dinner yet."

"Well, will you please do it anyway," Barry replied, in a low warning tone.

His voice gave her an ominous chill, and she was quick to comply with his wishes. "Very well," she said in an icy tone. "You seem to have the upper hand just now."

"Just now and from now on," Barry assured her. He had an air of cold ruthlessness about him that was now even apparent to Annie's parents. Annie could see the look of shock and surprise that passed from her mother's face to her father's. She trembled slightly, spilling her coffee onto the holiday linen tablecloth.

Turning her attention to the boys, Annie said, "After dinner, you must get ready for bed. Then your Grandfather will come upstairs and read to you."

"Will you, Grandpa?" Patrick asked.

"Indeed So." The elder gent assured the child. "As one Patrick to another, that's the very least I can do."

Patrick's brother turned to daddy and said, "I'm named Michael after your father, aren't I?"

"Yes, son that's true," Barry told him.

"But he's dead, huh?" the boy asked in a way that caused a ripple of laughter to float around the table.

"Yes, he died long before you were born. At any rate, later tonight I'll fix you guys some popcorn and we'll watch some TV together."

"Oh' boy!" Michael shouted enthusiastically.

"More turkey, dear?" Annie asked politely.

"No, I'm not hungry anymore." His face was abruptly flushed and he felt himself perspiring. He and Annie were unexpectedly drawn apart as he swore under his breath slightly and ungraciously left the table.

'What's wrong, Barry?"

Automatically, his expression grew cold and he stomped out of the room as he tried with much effort to tame his emotions. But is hampered by the awkward moments when he quickly grows ill.

"That man has a caustic tongue and around the children!" her mother observed with obvious disapproval. "I can't imagine what powers he has over you. Why, he's got you as nervous as a tweet? Why don't you pack up some things for yourself and the boys? Come stay with us for a while till he comes to his senses."

Annie, no longer able to disguise her discontent, asked her father to take the children for an evening walk while there was some sun light. "So that mom and I can talk," was her way of explaining it.

"Sure, Pumpkin, come along boys. Let's take the dog for a stroll through the grassy park." The kitchen door slammed shut over the sound of the clock's whirrs.

"Look, honey," her mother said in a soothing whisper, "You've had problems with him before..."

"It's true; Mom and I've long since accepted the fact that it's not part of his nature to be faithful to one woman for long." "So, you say now but maybe he's fallen in love."

"How would he even find the time to manage it? He works long hours, long weeks. The job makes ridiculous demands on him.

There's never any free time -"

"He must want it that way."

"I don't know what he wants. In any case, even though I hate him at times, I won't sit here and strip him entirely of any sense of loyalty."

FRANK VERDUZCO LOPEZ

"And I admire that in you, Annie. Even so, your father and I will be leaving soon. You know where to reach us, we're always glad to have you and boys over."

"Calm down, Mom. Remember, it's Thanksgiving. Can I get you another cup of coffee?"

"No, and stop changing the subject. We want to help you, dear, if only you'll let us."

"Look Mom, I'm not dragging the kids anywhere. They love him too much. And he loves them; you can see that, can't you?"

"So, now you're on his side," her mother said accusingly.

"I just don't want to use the children," Annie insisted stubbornly.

"Well, why won't you see an attorney at least? And get his professional opinion on things?"

"Don't you believe I love Barry?" Annie cried, in a voice nearly hysterical.

Her mother did not respond. She expresses great concern for her in view of her obvious distress.

"Well? Aren't you going to say anything? You mean you don't have any more questions?"

"Annie, I'm only trying to protect you. It's a mother's right, at least give me that." After a moment of silence, she added anxiously, "Are you okay, look at me."

"Yes, I mean no. I don't know anymore."

As her face grew pale and clammy to the touch, she quickly moved toward the bathroom, with her mother close behind.

Vomiting into the toilet bowl, Annie felt at once vulnerable and totally destroyed. At least the day was destroyed for Barry too and he ruined it for everyone.

"Oh God," Annie cried weakly, between long gasps, and is prompted to confess that she is expecting a child and admits that Barry is unaware of her condition.

"Ann, listen to me," her mother instructed. "You can't go on like this! Why haven't you told him you're pregnant?"

"To save my marriage!" Her entire lifestyle is beyond anything her mother could ever hope to understand. Turning the faucet on, Annie dampened a washcloth and applied it to her forehead. She sensed that her mother's eyes were boring into her, and that the rest of this conversation could not be avoided.

"Frankly, I think he's a perfect bastard, Annie. I don't think he gives a damn about you or the rest of the family."

"Please don't say that, Mom. And let me handle things in my own way. I'll say what needs to be said when the time is right. I know things have gone from bad to worse, but it will all work out. You'll see then I'll tell him about this baby."

After her mother had rummaged through the medicine cabinet, she pulled out a bottle of Maalox and told her daughter to take some. "Then I want you to lay down and rest," she said. "I'll clean up the kitchen."

"Thanks, Mom," Annie said gratefully and felt the color coming back into her cheeks. "Barry is a good man! He works hard and extra hours to put away money for the kid's college fund - so later we won't have to deliver pizzas or groceries to help them." This was no shared victory dance as her mother throw her hands up in the air.

For now, Barry was so entangled with a glamorous model in more troubling ways and must bear the burden no matter the cost. But nothing went as scripted, Lieutenant Bloodworth was a nasty thorn on his Achilles heel. He now grappled with this terrible thought. At one's glimpse it showed flashes of events yet to come his way willing to pay the bagpiper for duty, flag and country. but he was willing to pay the bagpiper for duty, flag and country.

THE COVER GIRL

CHAPTER 16

THE SKY WAS calm over the busy street as people on their way to work tried to dig out of the winter storm. The snow continued to swirl down over New York City, adding to the ground cover that was already five inches deep. Amid the season's first snowfall, December 1 ushered in a mild depression. At this time of year, the police suicide hotline work overtime and workers were busier than normal. True to form, this holiday season caused many to over-react to everyday problems and conditions of loneliness. In the heavy morning rush hour, wearing her tan cashmere coat, JeZe Bella wades through a crowd of early shoppers. She pushed past windows decked out with confetti of green and red colored paper, bows and ribbons. Inside the modeling agency, bright red, white and pink poinsettias decorated every desk and dressing room vanity. The Red Agency had taken on the glitter and greenery of the Christmas spirit.

Waltzing in late at 9:05, JeZe Bella dashed out of the elevator, slightly breathless. She tried to slip past Elaine Gondi who was rather busy pulling out advertising sales reports and records for an agency review meeting in progress.

"Oh, JeZe Bella! I'm glad to see you. I desperately need a volunteer to help decorated the office lobby tree. I can't do it myself because I've got to get these briefings together for Cherry. Honestly! This meeting took me completely by surprise."

A few moments later, she was standing on a ladder, sprucing up a fresh cut Bavarian pine that stood ten feet tall. It took less than an hour for Jeze Bella to trim the tree, for the office girls all pitched in to hang the miniature ornaments of gold and silver.

As the weeks flew by it was the 20th, another chill weather day at the city precinct, police headquarters. Although the P.D. conference room was spacious and warm, every available inch of space was occupied-the floor as well as the chairs.

Perched on a stool in front of the room, the indomitable Chief Abraham spoke skillfully to evoke favorable responses and lots of lighthearted laughter.

"I'm aware you motorcycle officers sometimes face hazards," he said. "Particularly, when trying to ticket or arrest errant motorists, let's think about this!"

"For a fact, Chief," remarked one officer. "There have been times when drivers have tried to run me over."

"Well now, that's exactly what we're here to discuss," the Chief said, by way of acknowledging this statement. "Now that the yuletide season is upon us, there'll be a greater number of drunken, hostile drivers to contend with. Quite often, a scuffle will develop."

At this point, Barry's eyes melted into the floor as the Chief's own gaze settled upon him. But Brent, with mocking playfulness, shoved an elbow into Barry's side, in light of an incident that had recently happened to them.

"The biggest problem we have to face is lack of public acceptance," Chief observed. "Our fair-minded citizens don't realize that the main purpose is to reduce traffic fatalities. They think we should be out chasing murderers instead of issuing traffic tickets."

"Chief, we've reduced the fatality rate but they won't give us credit because the radar-equipped cycles intimidate people, although they help us deter reckless speeding dynamos"." One of the choir boys said.

"Well, rest assured, men, that our only goal is to arrest drunken drivers between Christmas and New Year's Day," the Chief reflected.

"I know that in a number of instances, I've just narrowly avoided being hit by one of those alcoholics."

"Stark's right! I've been injured twice since joining the city metro division in June of 2010."

"Yeah, Hank. But one of those times, your rear wheel skidded out from under you when you hit an oil spot in the street. Remember?" someone recounted over the police laughter.

"How could my sore butt forget that? I slid half a city block with cuts and scrapes, but I didn't miss any time off work."

"Let's hold it down now, men," the Chief urged. "As some of you know, yesterday Jansen wasn't so lucky dodging a drunk driver. When a car in the lane to his right pulled in front of him to turn left at 42nd street, Jensen tried to avoid it, but failed. The 800-pound bike and the car collided. He was thrown over the hood of the vehicle, receiving a broken collarbone. He'll be out for five or six weeks."

"Personally, chief," Brent said, "I feel safer on a motorcycle than I do in my own car."

"Which brings something to mind," the Chief retorted. "During an eight to ten-, or twelve-hour shift, you men may log up to as many as a hundred miles and a fair amount of revenue for the city. You can easily issue fifty to sixty tickets daily."

"Yeah, but I'd prefer to see some of that profit in our pockets sometime," said one officer.

"You men should be pleased that you got a 9.62 percent salary increase over last year."

"Some arbitrator we have. We should all have gone on strike."

"Well, there's always the grievance procedure," the Chief reminded them tersely.

"What good is it? They always change their priorities, life insurance one day and dental-care the next."

"Look, I didn't come here to argue about inflation," the Chief responded heatedly.

"Obviously."

"Okay, now settle down! I've called this meeting to inform you that despite the very low injury rate on the icy streets, all peace officers on the bike beat are required to attend a one-week seminar on motorcycle safety. This will involve rigorous instruction, various maneuvers and the proper way to handle a fall from your cycles.

"Is this voluntary, Chief?" one rookie cop asked.

"Didn't you just hear me say it was required? Now, step up here and sign this damned roster."

"Christ!" Barry griped. "Christmas is almost here and I haven't even paid for the five-year-Old's kindergarten tuition fee. Yet Annie can afford to buy all kinds of fancy cat and dog food for the family pets."

"Don't despair," Brent said. "You can always moonlight as a male stripper at the Pink Pony Go, Go bar. I hear those Chip & Dale guys rake in lots of easy bucks on ladies' night."

"Oh sure, Annie would really go for that, what with her lily Christian ways. And you know P.D. wouldn't stand for it either conduct unbecoming to an officer, and all that crap!"

"Well, if your wife is as strait-laced as you say, how come she lets you play around?" Brent asked with a quick smile, as they all filed from the conference room.

Two black officers looked at one another and laughed. "Say," one of them said, "Maybe she doesn't give a damn, because he's got plenty to go around isn't that right Barry?"

Overhearing the distasteful remark, the chief cringed. "Barnes, I overheard that flaky comment. Now, move it. Move quick," he said, with the authority of a Marine Sergeant.

"Chief, I don't think the men meant anything by talking junk about Barry Stark!" Captain Tanner said fully entrenched. "Yes, I'm on edge if only I could now put a dent in our murdering cop case?"

"Maybe soon we'll know something chief."

"Drunk or sober your undercover guys should be working the streets for information." He sounded like an incisive social critic as things had stagnated to a point.

"Yes, they've wasted no time spreading the word." Captain Tanner said, "we are on over drive."

"I want to know if there's any connection to one of my men." The chief's lips barely moved.

"Well, I'm devoted to avoiding mistakes."

"I hope that's not going to happen on my watch. I've never missed a day in my thirty-five years of service - not one. I've earned the right to my pension and big fat salary plus all the perks."

"I don't blame you there Chief."

"I expect less lip from our cops and more respect."

"We both have a messy job to do and must go after all the dirty cops harder."

"Notwithstanding the heat of an internal affairs investigation."

"Chief, the long story short much to do but fret!"

"Don't take it as gospel, captain." The Chief expected and had instructed his officers and the detective to do the necessary on their precinct turf - and all arrests must be strong enough to hold convictions in the court of law. With all answers, questions, motives and actions and no leeway for nothing but the truth. The view he took as an issue were the lies and the obstruction of justice... in the undertone there was no silver lining for the police chief to speak of.

But for Barry Stark in his unrelenting actions, dying was one way to change his life's path. A bitter-sweet betrayal meant a quick bullet to the back of the head or a not so nice bloody blade across the throat from a cop hater. It was late afternoon and Barry made a speeding motorist stop. "Mario Andretti! You know why I stopped you?" He joked and placed his weighty hand on her shoulder. The sheer pleasure scattered all her thoughts. Wanting something to hold on to, what could she now expect of officer Stark? He had bent his head down and she felt the heat of his double-mint gum breath on her face. This lady was now overcome by a new weakness from her head to her toes.

"Oh, my god! You are so beautifully hot, officer!" The woman lamented as though she had died and went to La, La land.

"Look, sister! I'm giving you a break this time. Just don't speed on my turf again or I won't be so nice the next time," Barry winked.

There was no police brutality to be found from this cop today. She had no idea how long they stood there on the busy street curb.

Barry had read her mind in a sexual way he leaned in to whisper. "I think you are pretty hot yourself."

She was now lost at sea over a dreamy cop without a life-jacket a raft to hold onto. Not knowing his hands were of a stone-cold killer. Still, she was caught like a dangling worm on a silver fish hook by a tall dark handsome man of the law. For a moment Barry just stood there ill at ease as she gave his hand a little squeeze before driving off.

However, Barry's day was not over just yet. Playing to his inflated ego like an unexpected gift, he got loud screaming cat calls and whistles from a cruising red Buick convertible, full of wild coeds on the prowl. Humorously Barry turned bouncing from one foot to the other with both his fists up in the air. Much as a price fighter who just won his first bout in the boxing ring. Straddling onto his motorcycle in a to-and-fro motion like a dog in heat he answered a police code 10-13 hold-up in process. With strobes and sirens blazing Barry Stark melted onto his Harley-Davidson, vanishing into the network of heavy traffic on the boulevard.

That evening at police headquarters Barry handed in his reports and citation log sheets before clocking out for the day. Standing in a long line with other cops up against the brick wall. He dropped his handcuffs and warm leather gloves on the floor. Bending over to pick-up the gear he bumped his buttocks up against the wall and almost fell forward on wobbly knees.

As a female officer smiled at him and said, "Are you O.K., Stark?"

"Yes! If you like getting your royal ass kicked by the wall, Rowlands." He clearly stated with a poker-face.

All the cops standing in line laughed at Barry's comical aspect. His closest buddy-buddies in the department pandered to indulge him.

"Barry it's better than dropping a bar of soap in the men's shower room," Rowlands said coquettishly.

"Careful, that's anal harassment around here. But I'll keep all of you guessing about my posterior, babe!" Barry replied in a slangy style and grabbed his hind-end.

"Anatomy was my favorite class in school, Barry. You well know! I've got a big crush on your booty." Rowlands remarked smart and rollicking.

At that moment he blushed, red faced as she had broken the silence to all their serious matters of the day.........

THE ACQUISITION
CHAPTER 17

WITH A CUP of strong black coffee in his hand and a newspaper under his arms, Tony Savage walked past several clerical secretaries in the office. The morning headlines of the paper emphasized the most recent street murders in the city.

"Where are you heading for, Tony dear?" one of the girls asked.

"None of your itsy-bitsy business," came his playful reply.

"Moe Taylor, you're a fantastic flirt," another girl noticed coyly

"I can't help it! I find that guy incredibly incredible, his fair complexion features and deep blue-gray eyes-wow!"

"Funny thing, imagination, how it embellishes everything," Elaine responded with a teasing smile. As Moe moved to pick up a small clock on her desk, as if to throw it, Elaine mockingly ducked and said, "Just kidding, Moe."

It was 6:00 a.m. and the dawning light filtered slowly through the penthouse windows of the modeling agency. Behind a large round ivory-white desk, Cherry sat, dressed all in red, with an equally red telephone sitting at her elbow. A halo of silvery hair swirled around her face. Her hands, seemingly warped by age, picked up an 8x10 glossy. "Yes, JeZe Bella has that special Cover Girl look all right-the brilliant smile, the pearly white teeth and healthy head of shining blue-black hair."

In a moment of silence, she and Tony exchanged looks.

"Well, Tony darling," Cherry continued at last, "Are you just going to sit there? This is what you've been slaving for these months. My modeling agency has finally been awarded the Cover Girl makeup contract for a year-providing we use JeZe Bella Reyes face." She rose to her feet, with a spot of color brightening her cheeks. "Are you listening to me, Tony? I'd like you to break the good news to JeZe Bella."

"I'm sorry," Tony said, "I'm afraid I was thinking of something else."

"There is nothing else on earth. Come, come my top photographer. You should be very pleased with yourself darling man."

"Never mind what I am. What business is it of yours anyway?"

"Tony, what in the world has gotten into you? You're so angry and sullen when you should be on top of cloud nine. What's the matter, are you afraid she won't need your services anymore?"

"Shut up, Cherry, I don't have to take that from you."

"Ah, I see I've struck a raw nerve. Well, you've only yourself to blame if you let her walk off with some raunchy mouth cop. By nature, she's not an ingrate. Perhaps you should remind her where her true loyalties rest. And don't try to tell me you don't lover her. I've seen those looks. Why else would you be working so hard to make her a top model over the other girls?"

"Cherry, I really don't want— "

"What you really don't want is to wind your life the way I have with only a career. It can be quite empty and lonesome at the top. Take it from one who knows."

"Perhaps," Tony said, and emitted a weary sigh. "Look Cherry, I've got to go now and touch up a few more negatives."

"Oh, leave it be. Today's the day of our office Christmas party. Nobody will get any work done-except for our Elaine, of course. She's so dedicated."

Slipping past Tony, Moe came in through the red door, carrying a tray with a cup, saucer and coffee pot. She placed it on Cherry's desk along with a creamer, sugar bowl, and a small bottle of aspirin and a glass of water.

"Playing cupid?" she asked with a Texas drawl, once Tony was beyond earshot.

"So, you overheard us. Well, I hate to see him so upset at the thought of losing his favorite model over some ruffian in a uniform."

"Why, good golly, that would be a break."

"Oh Moe, don't be so rotten."

"I don't mean to be. But what Tony needs is a marrying settle down type of gal. One he can lasso willingly."

"On a hunch, would you be that filly so hot to trot in my very own agency?"

Moe's eyes widened ever so slightly. She turned and walked stiffly to the door, feeling her feathers a little ruffled.

At 9:00 a.m. Ronnie Love stepped from the elevator and met Jeze Bella's anxious gaze. "Ready for another Christmas party?" she asked.

"As ready as I'll ever be," JeZe Bella said with little enthusiasm. "Are you still in love with that cop? You're smiling."

"Yes, smiling but not saying a word."

"Sorry, I just wondered. I'm not trying to rub salt in the wound." Ronnie Love entered the office with her armful of small wrapped packages and placed them quickly under the tree. By late afternoon, the entire building was in a state of total disorder. Private Secretaries and their bosses were locked behind various doors, engaging in all sorts of pleasurable mayhem. Office staffs from different companies and floors comingled, adding their share of special jubilance to the holiday festivities.

As the girls gathered around the office tree, the excitement began to mount over the pile of brightly colored packages. In time, they un-wrapped all the gifts they'd exchanged, cluttering the room with debris of ribbons and glittering paper.

"One more party to endure before January 1st, "JeZe Bella said to Cherry, as she sampled some of the food platter's treats and alcoholic beverages.

"By the way, your cranberry relish is just tops!" "

"Try Elaine's mince pie. You'll like that even better."

"Do I dare?"JeZe Bella wondered aloud as she sipped her cup of punch. "JeZe Bella, come let us see what Santa brought you!" Maria teased. "Or is it a guilty secret?"

Picking up a beautifully wrapped large gold expensive looking box, Jeze Bella's eyes were nervous and questioning. Maria looked from Tony's angry face to hers, drawing her own conclusions.

"Please open it, JeZe Bella!" the other girls pleaded, and after a long moment she did.

JeZe Bella knew how to look wide-eyed, sensuous and amazed, which was the only way she could have looked, under the circumstances, as she held up a full-length fur coat, mink. The girls oohed and aahed, and JeZe Bella turned to Tony.

"What can I say, Tony? It's simply gorgeous! It's exactly what I've needed to complete my winter wardrobe."

"Say you'll have dinner with me tonight," Tony said, and smiled.

"How could she dare say no?" Moe Taylor asked, and everyone laughed.

JeZe Bella returned Moe's jealous gaze with a somewhat unfriendly one as Cherry said, "Why Tony, you're timing really surprises me. Why didn't you let me know this morning? This fits in perfectly."

"I don't understand what all this is about,"JeZe Bella interrupted then, "But then, I don't really care. Right now, I could kiss you, Tony. But I have a sore throat."

"Don't worry, you won't always have it," Tony said with a smile that crinkled the corners of his eyes. "I can wait."

By evening, the sleet and snow had left the roads encrusted with ice and slush. Meanwhile Barry Stark's life now read like a modern surreal satire, a gut-wrenching noir that could be torn from yesterday's news clippings that plunges deep in the morality of the glittery façade of the city. Where the crime scenes are nothing but! Barry Stark is engrossing and disturbing as the murders slowly accumulated, colder than ice a man that had spun-out of control. In the back ground noise, listening to his police broadband radio with emotions that were blown away like dust to the wind. Barry could be at times empathetic but never sentimental, he could be something wonderful and exceptional but then swallow oneself whole. He could steal the hearts of women and manages to be ebullient gripping. A testament to his formidable gift of good protocol as he takes an exuberant ride through the boroughs of the city with a white-hot passion. Asserting powerful obsessiveness for duty in the undertow of the bloody past that he could not outrun or escape. His life always hanging in the balance and jealousy in an unjust male-dominated world that drove him to his limit. Brash and unapologetic about the police brotherhood, whether working, drinking or laughing over his own difficult childhood.

Now standing at the cusp of doubt and destruction, threatening the balance of nature he feels expendable over his long-buried resentment that soon rises to the surface. That he did not see coming and could not shed the brainstorm in his head. With a wife calm and a demeanor of efficiency, he now stood at the crossroad of his marriage as a caged-up animal. Looking in the mirror he didn't recognize the person staring back, wanting to be invisible between a demanding career and raising a young family. He had lost his sense of self when something new needed to change like the unraveling of his marriage. Barry believed he was a good husband and a police officer with a myriad of duties. Seeing through different eyes his discontent comes into a sharp focus no longer willing to be anchored to home life. He regrets his failing marriage and family he once cherished. All his dreams were set adrift however harrowing no triumph of the human heart. Riding his motorcycle toward the heart of the city he thought about his kids. He hoped they were getting along alright in their catholic preschool. Yet there was a shadow that laid beneath his perception of home that was not a figment of his imagination.

As a new onslaught of weather plagued the city, the rank odor of uncollected garbage filtered through the air. With the strike by private sanitation workers going into its third week, the streets were infested with a mountain of refuse on every side. Making a life affirming decision with the approach of the Christmas Holiday, the acquisition of the exclusive contract with cover girl cosmetics is finalized. JeZe Bella Reyes is formally chosen as the model for their products and once again relies heavily upon the photographic genius of her close friend, Tony Savage, to present her image in the most favorable light. It was an ornamental evening. JeZe Bella's opulent body was attired in black velvet knickers and a captivating blouse, embellished with metallic ribbons and puffed ruffle sleeves.

Uptown, in the subzero temperature, like a cuddling couple turning heads, they stepped into a glass elevator and soared upward in a manner that left both her and Tony Savage slightly breathless. Looming through the mist was a spectacular view of the city's Christmas lights atop the towering buildings.

Strutting into the Tiffany-lit chalet dining night-club room, JeZe Bella allowed herself to be seated in an upholstered booth, and swayed seductively toward her escort as the drapes were neatly closed for privacy.

"Get us," Tony said, over a cocktail. "You're going to make a tidy sum from this Cover Girl makeup contract."

"Yes, and I'd be wise to invest my earnings," JeZe Bella mused as she eyed the lavish platters of pastries and the tempting array of hot hors d'oeuvres from the buffet tables.

"You're being all too logical, JeZe. I must say I'm pleased."

"Then I take it that it doesn't sound wrong to you?"

"Heavens, no after all, a penny saved is still a penny earned."

"My, my- what have we here, a poet laureate?"

"Hardly," Tony said with a chuckle. "It's all too trite, phrases, but there's still a great deal of truth in it."

"Well, I won't pretend, Tony. To me, money is everything. And yet, how sad that Sunday summons Monday, the start of yet another long work week for me."

"But not for long," Tony assured her. "You'll soon be part of the idle rich."

"Do you think so? How quaint. I can hardly wait."

"I only hope you're ready for it."

"Well, I won't be complaining about the Con Ed bill," JeZe Bella retorted snidely. "Besides, it's true that security has always been my primary concern, Tony. It's what I've worked for, prayed for-the only thing I've ever felt was really worth having!"

In the multi-level atmosphere of casual elegance, they danced to live music and dined on the finest gourmet cuts of two New York steaks. By 8:30 p.m., they were seated inside the club's cocktail lounge, drinking pink champagne and listening to an entertainer, a stand-up comic with a host of unbearable ethnic jokes, who was followed by the unparalleled sounds of a big black jazz singer.

"JeZe, your heart, along with your ambition seems to be somewhere else," Tony noticed with a gentle kind of bite.

"Come-off-it, Tony. You sound as if you were jealous of Barry Stark." There is a long, significant silence between them before she selected her words cautiously. "You could hardly equate the two security and Barry Stark."

"Well, why shouldn't I sound that way? I am jealous. I was afraid it was something more serious."

"How could it be?" JeZe Bella counters, "He's married as everyone knows."

"That never stopped anyone, before!"

"And here I thought I'd solved everything by having dinner with you tonight."

"Well, of course, I'm delighted that you did, I guess I'm being childish. Or, maybe I'm even being an idiot of the worst kind."

Emotionally charge, feeling lost and longing, she is unwittingly link to Barry by their hunger for a raw reckless physical attraction to one another. Throughout the dinner, Tony regards her closely. Outwardly, it appears that she has divested herself of whatever charismatic charm Stark has previously held for her. But there is something too flippant, too strident in her voice to appear entirely sincere.

"Look, Tony. Cheer-up it was only a brief interlude. Not at all in keeping with your usually moralistic character, please, could we call it a night now? I'm really tired; we've both have had a very long festive day."

"And I suppose I'm more than a little drunk too. Liquor can make you say stupid things." He sounded at a loss.

"It doesn't matter now," she said soothingly. "Let's go now; I can hardly hold my eyes open under these dim lights."

They concluded the evening by leaving the club in Tony's new LTD.

Across the street, in the dead silent shadows, Barry Stark stood, waiting and watching the dark windows of JeZe Bella's townhouse condo. He had been there for more than two hours, waiting in vain, but at last she finally arrived.

Even at 3:00 a.m. she continued to sparkle caught between give and-take, she leaned up against the inside of the car's door, pausing momentarily to rearrange her long hair and apply fresh lipstick.

"It's been great fun, Tony," she said.

"Life could be worse, JeZe!"

"Please," She said, as he sought to restrain her, "I really must go."
  "Let me come up for a while. I have not seen the new place yet"
"It's so late."
"But didn't you say you had a small gift to give me?"
"I'll give it to you around eleven o'clock," she parried. "That's a far more reasonable hour of the day."
"But I'm curious."
"Yes, I can see that, well so you won't lose any sleep over the matter, I'll tell you what it is. A pair of gold cufflinks so delicate, and exquisite for your silky white shirts, you'll love them, now then, pleasant dreams."
"Well, you can just bet that I'll be back at eleven," he assured her with a devilish grin and swiftly drove off into the early morning.

For one deadly moment, Barry stood frozen still on the icy ground, eyeing JeZe Bella as she turned and hummed a tune: LOVE IS HERE AND NOW YOU'RE GONE. The night had brought on a festive like celebration dinner; Tony and JeZe Bella toast one another and discuss the prospects of international success and what this could mean in terms of her future security.

Smoldering in his impenetrable handsomeness, a turbulent sexual jealousy now erupted in his cold murderous mind. Tacitly encouraged, he abruptly mounted his 800-lb. motorcycle as a stabbing pain shot through his throbbing temples. He bent down slowly, and hooked back up the wires to the police radio. His eyes squinted wearily as the dispatch calls started filtering through the air once again.

Across town, where Tony Savage lived, the apartment back corridor had been left ajar. Like a night hawk on the prowl, Barry walked one flight up the pitch-black stairway. The .38 magnum gun in his holster felt heavy with blind justice so he just took it out and held it cocked. Turning the doorknob, he entered the darken room. Under his feet, the old carpet had a musty film developer smell. The walls in the room seemed covered with endless photographs of faceless women.

Enveloped in his subconscious, Tony went to work emerging some time later from his lab darkroom. With newly wet processed 8x10 photos of JeZe Bella in a variety of nude poses. Suspended from the end of a clip, like meat on a sharp hook, "Well!" he says, by way of voicing his secret fears aloud, "Miss Reyes, once you're somebody famous, these pictures will insure that you will never be able to leave me, You've been talking a good little game but just in case you can't stick it out, I think I've got the ultimate persuader." While a threatening tone hung in the air, he stood in complete shadow with the red filter light glowing at his back.

When the unexpected happened, Barry grabbed him from behind and spun him around with a revengeful purpose. "Not-so fast," A voice calls out, "The best persuader is being pointed at you!"

Tony turns slowly to find himself staring into the grim face of Barry Stark, who is holding a cocked revolver.

"What in hell! You're that cop! Look, put that gun down. I could have you busted for this break in, Stark!" Tony sounded vindictively.

"Busted! I don't think so, Savage, why you got a few seconds to say your prayers." Barry shouted in the white heat of his anger.

"Look, man! What is this all about?" Tony said.

"Are you brain dead? Give me the negatives and those pictures, you bastard." Were his pitiless words showing no mercy?

"Sure...Sure. It's not what you think."

"Blackmail, that's what you're all about, scum-bag." Barry replied in a scathing commentary.

"What? No! I took these pictures a long time ago. When JeZe Bella was just getting started."

"Now you are using them for insurance in case she gets some ideas. You're a real pal, Savage. It must make you feel great to have her tell all the newspapers and TV Reporters what a great guy you are" Barry stated implicitly.

"You've got the story all wrong, Stark!"

"Then start talking, and make it quick, your time is so running out."

"Stark, listen to me! Getting rid of me isn't going to help you. She told me she is through with you for good."

"So what in the Hell are those nudie pictures for? To make sure things stay the same way between the both of you."

In a last ditch effort, Tony cries. "Okay, yes! I know her she's basically level-headed but she's emotional too, even impulsive at times. JeZe Bella doesn't always know what's best for her until I came along and saved her from herself."

"But you do?"

"That's right. It's true what she said about my part in her career. She wanted fame. I help give it to her. She wanted security. I've given her that too."

"How perfect, if she only wanted you. But she doesn't because Jeze Bella has her designs on only one man and here I stand right between you and her."

"Stark, you don't understand my relationship with JeZe Bella..."

"I know it's not going anywhere and that's what those pictures are really for. Not to keep her away from me- -but to keep her with you! Any way you can, isn't that right Savage!"

"No! No! You cannot shoot me, man." He fell to his knees. A shot is heard and Tony reels to his feet, as if he is fatally wounded. Then, as Barry Stark approaches him, Tony Lunges toward him and they grapple on the floor until Barry positions himself properly in order to apply a professional choke-hold. Rendering his victim unconscious, Barry regains control of himself in time to realize that he must make this look like an accident. The bullet had only grazed Savage's head; Barry quickly douses the room with liquid developer and then sets the chemical ablaze like a Molotov cocktail. Whereupon the entire room bursts into a flammable hell as fire engines and police sirens respond to a three-alarm fire in Queens, quietly Barry Stark vanishes into the compelling night.

In the heat of the fire, Tony came to and heard the crackling of flames, and then he smelled the smoke. Kneeling on the floor, he tugged at the door to escape the flames that spat and hissed at him. His eyes were burning from the thickening smoke. As the flames raged up the stairwells and were sucked out the front doors. It was a hellish blaze to fight as a team of ladder men crashed through the entrance and ran up the first flight of stairs to knock out windows for purposes of ventilation.

"I'd like to get hold of that pyromaniac," a red-faced choking fireman protested.

"Yeah, that lousy son-of-a-bitch," a second man shouted hoarsely.

In the three- alarm the fire chief's car gleamed red under the streetlamp as a police car rushed in from the side alley in the noisy rescue. Fire engines with crimson bubble lights were summoned from all corners of east Queens, the fire rigs lined the street for blocks as the spinning red lights glared off the wet pavement. It turned out to be a code one-death. The others codes meant injuries, serious to critical.

The radio cracked at the mercy of the intrepid Fire Marshal's loud Irish brogue. "One 1045 code confirmed, ten-four." Many people poured into the street, stepping over the high-pressure fire hoses that had been brought into play.

Once again, the agitated voice of the Fire Marshal said, "Everyone back. Please move away from the area."

Fireman carefully aided men, women and children who were overcome by the smoke, giving them mouth-to-mouth resuscitation. The building was completely gutted; a cry came through the gaping entry-way, where the figure of a man stood atop the hall stairs. He had found his retreat blocked by a wall of flames.

There was the taste of acrid smoke in the air. The man groped through the dead zero visibility and was trapped. The fire curled around the steps and old timbers, making it impossible for the staircase to support his weight.

"Somebody please help me!" he sobbed, as the whole stairway collapsed from under him. He fell into a cascade of fire and was quickly lost from sight in the burning timbers.

On Christmas Morning, the three-alarm fire had destroyed the old apartment complex. More than 100 firefighters controlled the blaze. Within sixty minutes' time as New York metro firemen poured up to 2,000 gallons of water a minute on the fire in order to control it from spreading to other buildings. Finally, the bloody flames came to an end of cinders as the dawning light approaches.

These horrible fires shock the city that was already on the edge. The Metro Chief of Police must now decide what action to take behind the true nature of the fires. The stage was set for another investigation that Chief Abraham did not need or wanted

WINDOW OF HOPE
CHAPTER 18

TONY SAVAGE WAS moved to Kings County Hospital by ambulance: he was moved more dead than alive. Once there, he was taken to the extensive burn unit, where his condition was listed as critical. On a day after Christmas, JeZe Bella was made to understand that he was dying, even though he appeared to be stable. From the hospital window, JeZe Bella looks out onto the street life. For several hours, Tony Savage's life hangs by a thread and she maintains a constant vigil by his bedside.

"Miss Reyes, I'll be frank with you," Dr. Higgins said. "My patient, Mr. Tony Savage, is bleeding through his catheter and is not expected to live but for now he is heavily sedated and unable to see any visitors."

Her gazing eyes quickly focused on the bed to the right with a large drawn curtain around it. She looked at Tony, and saw his torso was thickly-muscled and there were tattooed serpents inked on his biceps. He had tousled blond, brown hair; his face was strong and handsome as she remembered it. But now he was swathed in bandages, his blue-gray eyes were swollen shut. She now had caught the unmistakable pungent odor of burned human flesh.

On the following Days, she learns that his condition has deteriorated and is not expected to live. JeZe Bella attempts to see him but is refused admittance until he rallies suddenly and starts asking for her by name.

"Miss, just for a few moments..." the nurse advises her and JeZe Bella nods solemnly. She does not expect Tony to be conscious, or to know who she is, but there is a remarkably lucid quality about him now. A kind of frantic and desperation of a sick-man, that is taxing the last of his strength.

"Barry Stark!" he mumbles through thin, rigid lips.

"What did you say? Barry Stark!" JeZe Bella cries, "Oh! Oh! Tony."

"Be careful, JeZe Bella!... Be!" He whispers and goes unconscious. Jeze Bella's eyes immediately flooded with tears and she finds herself shrinking back away from Tony, away from the very possibility of such an idea. She recognizes in his words a thought half-formed...something someone else would have to tell her before she could ever admit it to herself. (Barry is a man very capable of this.)

The nurse re-enters to the room...leads JeZe Bella slowly away...asks if there is anything she can do.

"Do? No... there's nothing that can be done, now." She leaves the hospital and wanders the squalid streets in a directionless frenzy. Who would believe such an incredible story? What if Tony Savage were merely hallucinating? Did she dare risk Barry's career, his family, his children, over the incredible ravings of a critically burn man. JeZe Bella knew she would have given anything not to have heard Barry's name, to be burdened with his words and for all the rest of her days. There was the impulsive desire to run to escape the responsibility of having to do something about all this, to somehow act rationally in a totally irrational world. "Dear God, please don't let Tony die." She cries aloud, "The Doctors must be wrong this time. He's got to recover and explain what really happened-calmly, logically... And in a way that won't implicate Barry Stark."

With the approach of the New Year, a plan begins to formulate itself in her mind. It is as simple as running away going someplace where the problem does not exist. There was the quick phone call to her Boss, Cherry. The few, well-chosen words she is surprised to her Cherry refer to as (Mindless Gibberish.)

"What in the world are you suggesting? You can't just walk out! You have a responsibility to my Agency, to the fulfillment of our contract with Cover Girl. To the G-Girl, or have you forgotten?"

JeZe Bella responds with a listless laugh. "It was Tony's hard work that gave me what I have. Tony, who now will take it all away for it was only he who could make me the toast of the New York's electric billboards and it, is my entire fault."

"Good, God! What are you raving about? Pull yourself together. Those Docs don't know everything. Tony's fighting for his life. It's not over yet. The will to live is powerful if I know the man!"

"I just don't see it in the cards anymore, Cherry!"

"OK, just listen. If you pull out on me now, and void this cosmetic contract for this agency, I'll see to it that you never work in this town again."

"And I'm called a Bitch! Well, you see to it!" Click, click on the opposite ends of the cell phone, both woman stare at the dead instrument in their hands.

The news had been grim. Tony had lapsed into a deep coma from which there would be no recovery. JeZe Bella had been busy pasting pictures of herself into a pink scrapbook. She had hoped to be able to show it to Tony, but now, there was no longer any possibility of that. When JeZe Bella heard an incessant ringing of the doorbell pushes its way through the darkness of her thoughts. She moves to the door and admits Lieutenant Bloodworth, holding his badge out with a defanged smile.

"Going somewhere?" He asks, and nods significantly toward the two suitcases standing by the door.

"Say, you guys have worn that line into the ground." JeZe Bell retorts with a mirthless laugh, "I wonder if it ever occurred to you that a suitcase can mean that I may be returning from a trip just as easily as going on one."

"But in order to return from somewhere, you've got to go there first. That's the natural order of things."

"Anyway, tell me, Lieutenant what brings you out to my doorstep."

"The case of a horribly burned man, Tony Savage!"

"That's absurd, Tony happens to be very critical in the hospital, I've seen him almost every day since the horrific fire."

"Have you seen him today?"

"No! I was on my way there, but why all this questioning."

"Don't look so worried, he is not a patient anymore. And I am conducting an investigation. There is strong reason to believe that foul play is involved made to look like an accident or suicide." The Lieutenant moves forward quickly as JeZe Bella reels toward the nearest chair. After taking a few breaths, she manages to regain some measure of composure.

"How very cruel of you, what you just did."

"I'm sorry, but I had to see your reaction."

"I hope you weren't disappointed? Tony was my best friend so you are dashing down a blind alley coming to me for answers." "I'm a cop Miss Reyes and have you heard of obstruction of justice?"

"That's a poor excuse."

"You should be eager to see his murderer brought to justice."

"Well, how do you know it was murder?"

"If it wasn't arson, and it wasn't suicide. What would you think it was?"

"An accident...as as you said."

"Yes, and I'm Saint RamZ, in the flesh or should I say superman."

"What makes you so sure it wasn't?"

"That's what the investigation tells us. Now then, what do you know about any enemies he might have had?"

"None that I would know of, he was a very kind man and very professional."

"That's funny, your co-workers at the agency tell it differently."

"What friends?"

"I see. Savage had no enemies, and you have no friends."

"Look Lieutenant, if you mean the girls from the modeling agency- they're just people I work with."

"Still very observant people, claiming there was a man in your life who considered Tony Savage very tough competition. Anything you'd like to add to that?"

"Yes, the cherry Red Agency is not a reliable source of information about me; I'm not even seeing anyone for that matter. In fact, at the moment, it would be best to dismiss whatever they say on the basis of certain vindictiveness."

"Toward you may I ask?"

"Yes, I've terminated my association with the agency. I guess they didn't like the way I went about it. I guess I've had it up to here with them."

"But didn't I just read something about a million dollar contract-?"

"You can't always believe everything you read in the newspapers, Lieutenant. Now, please go and leave me alone. You've just dealt me some shocking news. I have the right to mourn the passing of Tony Savage in my own privacy."

"Of course, miss Reyes. But don't leave the city just yet!"

"I wouldn't dream of it but next time, bring a subpoena with you. If you would like to see me as a material witness," JeZe Bella says then, smiling sweetly.

"You don't want to commit a felony. That means not coming forward and telling all you know about a crime that has been committed."

"Technically, how could I be guilty? I mean, I'm completely in the dark."

"Miss Reyes, why do you want to mess up your life?"

"My life, you say? Why, I don't have one now. The only chance to be something is gone, along with Tony Savage. All that is left is a nice scandalous statement tinged with sex.' "

"Sounds quite sordid, I can almost savor it with the gusto of a fine connoisseur," he said, with a leering stare.

"I didn't have the luxury you would think I've had. Let's say I ran from a pimp. Once, I left the Sunset Strip in Hollywood California, by way of LAX, on the first 747 jetliner to paradise." She spoke with mocking ridicule. "See, I was then being relaxed and pampered aboard a fabulous cruise ship. That was sailing from Honolulu to the sun-blessed island ports on Maui, Kauai and then to Sidney, Australia. When I first met Tony Savage seated on a lounge chair, next to mine. This trip was meant to be my last journey. You see, when the money ran out, I was going to commit suicide. But Tony came to my rescue. He convinced me to come to New York with him and no strings. He was a free-lance photographer at the time. Funny, I guess he pitied me and vowed he could make me somebody."

"Suddenly, Miss Reyes, you can dream up your past, but you can't answer my simple questions."

"Exactly, I'll level with you, Lieutenant. I'll tell you something more about JeZe Bella Reyes. I usually lie to anyone I meet except Tony, who knew the truth about me." Like a flashback of her twenty-three years, she reached into a gold jewelry box on the mantel of the fireplace and handed him a clipping out of an old newspaper.

"I keep it to remind myself from whence I came," she said with a sad smile.

The newspaper photo showed an old grey-haired wino beside a garbage can in the park. A related article explained that he had discovered a tiny four-pound infant in a shoe box dumped in the trash bin.

"I'm sorry, Miss Reyes, but surely you don't have to let the past haunt you like this, we all have something to hide."

"Why not, you don't know the half of it. As you can see, I was dubbed Pandora's baby because of the label on the box-Shoes by Pandora. I was left to die," she explained, a trifle vengefully, "By a heartless mother whom I never knew. My birthplace was a trash bin in a run-down park on the island of Puerto Rico. I never had a real mother or a father-just the details of my unfortunate beginnings in this clipping."

"But you were found. Shouldn't you be grateful?'

"Grateful, is that what you think I should be? Well, here's the low-down. I was adopted by a young couple who couldn't have children of their own, and when their marriage didn't work out, I went back to the orphanage. Then, there was a second couple who sent me back once they'd managed to have a child, and the third couple was the worst experience of all. You see, I was a mature twelve-year-old by that time, and my new stepfather rape me. He went to jail for what he did and my stepmother blamed me. Again, I went back to the orphanage. So one day I ran away for a whole year, living on the streets. But then they found me and put me in a girls' reform school. Look, I don't want you to feel sorry for me. That's not why I'm telling you this. You'll never hear me whimper about any of it. It's past and done. Now ... as for the present, if you can prove anything, you'd better have a squad of the best prosecutors ready to try and make it stick, because I'm not afraid, I've got nothing more to lose."

The Lieutenant eyed the floor a moment, and then chose his words carefully. "If I can confirm what you told me, there won't be anything for you to worry about Miss. Reyes."

"All I can ask is that you please be discreet in checking out my story."

He put his notebook away and stood up. She walked him to the door and they shook hands, formally.

"Lieutenant, don't hesitate to call me, I've done nothing wrong."

"Yes, a case like this one is exceptional. It's a matter of finding a witness who will talk. We have to proceed very carefully because it's not an open-and-shut crime but murder as I have deep feelings."

"Apparently if you can manage to solve this crime, I just want to live a normal life if I can from all that has happened."

"You will rest assure, we already have one confession from a crank. They show up out of the wood work, he's willing to confess to anything, including arson. Fire bugs, a torch for hire. If it's true, what he knows could put others behind bars."

"Lieutenant, you don't mean he could be an arsonist-for-profit. It is some tip-off and I am very glad to hear this."

"I shouldn't discuss the case with anyone, but the sellers and buyers were in conspiracy with him. He told me all about it— how the buildings would change hands five times to escalate the insurance they would collect. And the apartment building has had several owners, but the man has had a case history of mental problems. Because of this, what can we do? A jury would laugh us out of court."

"After this, I'm afraid I don't hold that special gift and excitement for New York I once did."

"Understandably, I guess I've learned to bad-mouth the city as ood as anyone, still I can't imagine myself living anywhere else on the planet."

"Well, goodnight, Lieutenant and good luck." And once he had one, her smile remains a rehearsal. For many, such smiles to come. Tony's death and the many horrible implications connected with it worked relentlessly to break her spirit. For it was last night, Tony Savage died all alone, precisely at 11:59 p.m., just days before the New Year. The fire investigator never got the admissible deathbed statement, or the identity of the arsonist attacker.

It was December 30th; Annie was planning the evening meal in the kitchen while Barry napped on the couch in front of the six o'clock television news. As he slept, it blared out the news of the latest arson wars in New York City during these cold winter months. When the phone rang, Annie moved quickly to answer it.

"Hello, Annie, this is Constance. I called to wish you and Barry a very Happy New Year. I miss not seeing since the Christmas Mass."

"I was so surprised to turn and see the familiar faces of you and Brent," Annie told her. "I remember, it was when the service was just starting."

"Yes, Brent and I recognized the boys Patrick and Michael right away. It was comical to watch them pulling in different directions in the front pew. But that's not the reason I called. I was wondering if you and Barry could drop by a little later for a few HNY cocktails."

"I don't think that would be wise," Annie said. "The fact is, Barry's been in something of a drunken stupor for the past few days. It really put a damper on things over the holidays. Still, it seemed best not to subject him to a swarm of relatives after the way he behaved on Thanksgiving."

"Oh Annie....I'm so sorry to hear that. Did you really have a miserable Christmas?"

"I'm afraid so...not only because his gift to me was so inexpensive, but because of his lack of feeling for me."

"Well, don't judge him by that. All men hate to shop. I know Brent does, even for himself. They've somehow never mastered the art of it. At any rate, just think of Barry as a store-shy husband. That should pacify your feelings somewhat."

"I suppose so," Annie agreed. "A personal gift can't reall compete with one's love for someone. All in all, things didn't turn out too badly. Before Barry went on duty at midnight, we watched a Christmas special and enjoyed a large bowl of buttered popcorn, that Barry popped himself."

"Barry's a helluva cop, and it's sad, but he didn't have to volunteer for that particular shift. There are plenty of single guys on the force who could have filled in."

"Look, Constance, he's a cop and always will be. He hangs out with cops, he talks like a cop, and he acts like a cop."

"Aha, I detect a note of defensiveness," Constance said with a laugh. "Remember, Annie, I'm your friend. And speaking as one, Barry should be told at once, from your own lips, that you're three months along. Before someone else lets it slip out somewhere, and you end up being the deceitful wife."

"Excuse me, but I have to go now and Happy New Year." Annie tried not to sound agitated as she abruptly hung up the phone. For her, Barry and the kids this New Year's Eve will be enjoyed watching from in front of the big screen TV and not standing on Times Square ring in the New Year.

PATROLLING THE BOULEVARD
CHAPTER 19

DRIVING DOWN THE most renowned boulevard in the world, foreign cars filled with famous stars were glimpsed at glamorizing the latest show on Broadway. But under the magical neon-lit billboards on Times Square, an older profession scandalized the city, block by block. The sluts, idling on street corners so young, pretty, charming, and even affluent as some of the girls stood outside the La Paz Lounge, gazing into the traffic.

"Liz Estrada," Carolyn whispered, "Don't look now, but guess. who's on the night beat?"

"Yes, the white knight! He is one of the royal corporals riding past us on his steel cycle—a real roadblock to our only source of income and a real hazard to our profession."

"Still, he's quite a movement, shifting in all his manly directions," Carolyn said a trifle fancifully. "I have an idea I wouldn't mind the struggle but I have to make a living wage tonight."

"Well, I'd certainly decline the opportunity! Particularly after he attempted to arrest Lori Toy last month and broke her little arm in three places."

"I heard about that, Liz. How he placed a handcuff on her right wrist and was struggling to place one on her left."

"Look, I don't like the cop's outward stance of hostility against us," she said, bristling. "That was no accident; it was intentional police brutality. All he wanted was her money which he got."

"Look, girl we better stop this endless argument about raw force and get booking before our crazy pimp does the same kind of number on us tonight."

"Listen, Carolyn. I don't like your joke about our monkey-boss."

"I just dig Barry Stark; he's all man to me better than a stinking john."

These cops patrol of the busy street was on the night tour that cruised down Broadway BVLD. As they both approached the main intersection, auspiciously, they caught sight of five Puerto Rican juveniles flashing knives. Swiftly, Barry and Brent bounced off their gleaming cycles onto the side walk, forcing a path through the crowd with their black batons drawn.

"Drop the blades, punks!" Brent held his gun firmly as both hands tightened around the butt, and pointed it directly at their bellies.

Amid the gasping crowd, cell phone cameras everywhere the street-wise punks knew that the .38 magnum at point-blank range could drop a man dead in his tracks. Four of them immediately let their weapons clatter to the icy cement.

"Hey, hold it, you bastard!" Barry cursed at the top of his lungs.

"Who the hell are you, pig?" the fifth juv ignored the warning and fled around the street corner, instinctively retreating into the dark shadows.

"I'll grab that S.O.B.," Barry shouted and raced off after the young hoodlum. Halfway down the snowy street, he remembered to pull his gun, and then chase the punk two more blocks down a dark slippery stench-infested alley.

Barry caught up to him and threw a death arm choke hold around his neck, then stuck the magnum gun barrel in his ear.

"Let go of me, your honky motherfucker!" the kids' eyes were popping as the gun cocked. Barry was short of squeezing the trigger.

"I ought to waste you kid," he muttered angrily, but then, through their heavy breathing, he heard a siren whooping in the cold foul air. Hand cuffing his prisoner caused the kid to walk meekly back, in a dehumanizing way. He limped on a leg that had suffered a kick in the groin from the arresting officer. Back on the sidewalk, a patrol car with two officers from the local precinct slammed up to the side of the curb and disengaged the scene like a cavalry force.

As one big uniformed cop rolled down his window and stuck his head out, he asked, "Is everything under control, Brent?"

"You got that straight, Amboy. I'm watching them like a hawk." The young punks were all crouched down on their knees, holding their hands against the back of their heads.

"I'll help you load them into the police van," Amboy said while the radio dispatch blared out the 10-13 on the horn.

"Here's the other fledgling," Barry yelled from the street corner, to make himself heard. Unyielding and nearly impossible to handle, the young ruffian hopped and acted crazily.

"Remove his handcuffs, you bully," some protested in the confusion.

"The *Spick* is just bleeding a little," Barry said. His rough reputation no longer an illusion or his incendiary mouth.

"The baton again, Barry?" police Sergeant Romero asked.

"He's a tough street kid and resisted arrest," Barry explained scornfully. "And I didn't think twice about hitting him."

"Looks like you taught him a lesson," come's his ac-cussing retort. "Now, I'll have to take him down to city clinic with a cracked head."

"You want an official escort from brother officers?" Barry asked, a little less friendly, but Romero took the observation lightly, for he was a cop who had seen it all.

"Isn't there a limit to police brutality?" pleaded an old woman as the awful truth sank in. Distrustful of their own NYPD, the people in the crowd remained incensed that this dirty cop's story would hold up in an internal investigation.

"What's his cock-and-bull story going to be, Barry?" The fuming brown eyed sergeant asked.

"You speak the lingo, don't you, Romero?" Barry winked.

"Don't hassle me, Barry, I'm the good guy, remember?"

"Yes sir. And you can see the city is menaced with these knife hefting street gangs." With that, Barry looked to justify his own actions. By frisking the kid, and exposing the evidence, he was able to end the speculation in the heated crowd. He reached into the kid's jacket and pulled out a knife with a nine-inch blade that snapped out and locked into place.

"Holy-smoke and mother of Jesus, he's got a small sword!"

"It's typical for the night-prowlers that hit on the street drunks and hookers," Barry said gingerly, while the blade gleamed under the reflecting lights.

"Say, the handle has a panther emblem, a most prized knife at that."

"You bet, Sergeant!"

"Look, I've had a hard day. I don't intend to freeze my butt out here. I'll meet you later at headquarters along with your report officer Stark."

"Sure, Sergeant," Barry erupted loudly. "But I'd like to arrest that ugly so-of-a-gun over there, for peeing all over my new bike."

"How'd you like to bite on it, pig? The homeless drunk snarled.

"Just pull the family jewel out one more time buddy," Barry warned with antagonism, "And I'll shoot the god-damned thing off."

"Barry," Sergeant ordered, "Would you please mind getting out of here, and just leaving well enough alone?"

"Hell, these freaks should be in zoos," he fumed.

Emotionally, Brent pulled him away as his outrage swelled and before an argument ensued. "Okay, Barry! What do you say we go get us a cup of Joe and a couple of doughnuts, those crispy creams you like so much?"

"The show is over, folks!" Romero's pride as an officer and his frustration with the situation showed through his speech.

"You beat the kid savagely," a man lamented heatedly. "That takes an animal to do that to a young boy!"

"If we don't cover our ass, who, will?" Amboy replied in Barry's behalf, as Romero patted him on the back and the man's screams went unanswered. The gathering crowd stood around like robots New York had become emphatically stricken.

THE POWER OF LOVE
CHAPTER 20

NEW YORK, THAT place of so much promise, has lost its majesty, its beauty, its power-reflecting only the loneliness of too much too soon, and never quite enough too late. Inside Ralph's coffee dinner across the icy wet street from the Red Modeling Agency, JeZe Bella sat in the company of Lieutenant Bloodworth. They were lingering over hot coffee as the waiter came back to the table and refilled their cups, even as JeZe Bella declined a second cup.

"I'm looking for a new friend, Lieutenant. Do you know where I could find one?"

"That's a gloomy thought, Miss Reyes. It seems you are having a rough time dealing with Tony's death."

"Look, the hard fact is that the present line of questioning had gotten us nowhere. In actuality, it has only added conflict to both our lives."

"Well, a good criminal investigation always begins a case by suspecting everybody." The Lieutenant stirred with a compulsive snap to his speech. "Even daring hunches, we accept nothing at face value."

JeZe Bella raised a stony, tear-struck face and said, "Surely you're jumping to conclusions."

"Am I? The Metro fire investigator said there was deep charring on the floor." His voice quickened, as if to snare the scene with his words.

"That would tell us flammable liquid had been used. Would you guess a premeditated revenge strike against Mr. Savage?"

"Why, the very idea is inhuman!"

"Still, do you know if he had any personal enemies who might want to kill him? It's my own opinion that the fire was set deliberately."

"So, now it's a dangerous psychopath." She smiled thinly as he probed, poked, pushed and questioned her.

He found her answer elusive and the girl herself most unyielding. The exact story of what had happened in Queens the night of the fire remained shrouded in total mystery.

Walking back into the ornate and richly furnished office of the Red Agency, JeZe Bella came to gather her things looking unusually somber.

Eating her toast at her desk, Elaine took another bite and threw the rest into a paper sack. "JeZe Bella, at last you show up!" She said. "Are you okay and just to walk out on us?"

"Sure, Elaine, what's the matter? Why are you so worked up about my business?"

"You came in and left with a police lieutenant. Did he take you to the police station?"

"No, for heaven's sake, I wasn't being arrested." As she spoke, she tried to keep her hands from shacking.

"Well, I just wanted you to know I was concerned about you." Elaine put her coffee cup down and tilted back in her chair.

"It is very sweet of you, Elaine, to bother yourself over me." She held up a Xerox copy of a memo that Cherry had distributed to everyone this morning. Most of it dealt with a statement over the loss of the Cover-Girl contract and the problems connected with replacing Tony Savage and her.

"Do you suppose it was an accident? I'm still surprised he even lit a cigarette because he hadn't had a pack in months. After a struggle like that, he had a strong conviction, I would say."

Jeze Bella crushed the memo in her hand. Her warm smile disappeared at the memory. "This is pretty insane, Elaine. I can't make any commitments about my career until Tony's death has been cleared up."

"JeZe Bella, don't do this to you," Elaine insisted. "You don't want to windup selling beauty kits in some cheap department store someday."

"Bye, Elaine, I haven't the time to figure out if that would be a plus or a minus." She reluctantly drifted away, tucking a black lock of hair back in place as she departed. She was as low as she had ever been in her entire life. In deep remorse, and full of recriminating feelings, slamming the door behind her.

Lulu walked up and said, "Don't fret, Elaine, I'll see her later. We belong to the same Health Spa where we're both taking the same aerobic dance class."

"Oh, Lulu-here she is at dizzying heights, both admired and envied." Elaine shrugged. "But somehow, I feel we've seen the last of her to be very honest."

"Ha!" Maria, one of JeZe Bella's more acid rivals said. "She's no great loss here or anywhere."

"Funny, I don't feel that way," Cherry intervened from the back of the room before the nervous countenances of the office staff.

"Yes, you're just a vain mean bitch, Maria." Elaine managed to have the final clincher. "All one has to do is catch you with your mouth working overtime."

Caught in the patchwork of her evil tongue, with no mental reservations left, Maria lost all chance of escape. With no friends in sight, she broke down into tears.

In a fade from dawn to dusk, the night slickened forth as the neon lights spanned the inner city like flickering jewels. JeZe Bella sat patiently waiting inside the dark street corner bar known to many as The Paradise Lounge. The odor of beer and hard liquor breath hung in the air. Sipping on a glass of white rum, her personal preference, she was scantily clad in a tantalizing white Norwegian fox fur. Whiling away the time, she sat gazing out the door at the city towers. a graphically suggestive way, she crossed her legs, and was well aware that men were staring at her, but since these were only crude leers, she paid them no mind. Then a nice-looking, bald, middle-aged man made a taxing move around the crowed room. Noticing her, he immediately maneuvered himself over to her, unable to resist temptation. Lounging against the vinyl arm rest of her chair, JeZe Bella wore Expensive French cologne, leaving nothing to chance.

"Should I be warned about you?" the man asked, maintaining a tan glow.

"Do you mean that as a social criticism?"

"Please don't misunderstand me," he hastily amended.

"No chance of that. But then, that's the business we girls are in."

"Say, are you planning to leave soon?" he asked in the enticement. "I could be persuaded to stay. Still, if that scares you"

"No, wait!" the man said hurriedly, gathering courage. He tentatively restrained her with his arm.

"Look, Mr. whoever you are there is no man who could ever be generous enough to suit me."

"B-But I'm a doctor, I've never done anything like this before." "Like hell you haven't. So, show me the money." She asked coaxingly.

"Is your approach always so direct?"

She wisely put her arms around his neck and said in a whisper, "yes. One thousand dollars and don't tell me you can't afford it-doctor."

Quite against his will, he found himself giving in to her wishes. "You're very compelling, Miss"

"So I've been told plenty of times." With an appreciative laugh, she entwined her arm through his. "Shall we go?" moving through a small crowd at the doorway, they quickly departed, while a number of the patrons admired JeZe Bella's essentially marvelous, high process walk. It was truly professional; the kind of stride only macho-men could appreciate. But the nightmare of this long night would soon begin. Reverting to an earlier, self-destructive path, Jeze Bella explores the surface of that seething world of eroticism that grinds away. One could hear the harsh voices and coarse laughter in the place, which was nothing short of deafening. Amid the lost souls, the pornographic toilets, the great hungry groping for a moment of passion or high, the nightmare of this night would soon begin. As Barry Stark parked his motorcycle beside the street curb and decided to walk the beat. He strode his leather black boots to the sidewalk with his manly shoulders rolling back and forth. As he parted through the roving crowd, swing his big black baton in one hand with the ever-mocking authority of the Law.

Satirizing the hour, there was a calypso flavored kind of music that briskly filled the air. JeZe Bella waited, leaning up against the cold dark side of a building as splendid Cadillac's, and Mercedes Benz's slowly cruised the well-known block. She becomes a symbol of those things and those promises, in her black fishnet stockings and gaudy fur attire, until she foolishly rewarded the wrong person with the glow of her painted on smile a few hours ago. Whence she heard the striking of a baton on the wall behind her head, startled, JeZe Bella spun around. Along the graffiti wall, a monstrous shadow emerges from the dark murk. It is Stark, who steps out of the shadows, who pulls her into the light, who is momentarily transfixed in the shock of recognition, long enough to give her no chance for escape.

"Oh, hell! It would happen to be you, Barry Stark the cop?"

His response did not surprise her as Barry tapped the brim of his black and white helmet by way of an acknowledgement. "You seem surprised or a little shock at the sight of me, JeZe Bella or are we afraid I've misjudged you?"

"What if I do, this is none of your damned business. Besides I thought by now you'd found someone else to get those rocks of yours off." She replied callously.

"Meaning, apparently what?" he asked, striding in front of her with obvious agitation.

"Meaning that I think you are an arrogant dickhead to interfere in my personal affairs."

"Granted, but I carry a badge and gun. And I cannot condone your actions on the street," he snarled into her ear. "You're breaking the law, you cheap trick!"

"Don't be a common fool, Barry. If you want to start a quarrel, then say so."

It was in the heat of the moment that his image began to gnaw at her as he grappled aggressively with her lithe form, causing a small plastic bottle to flip out of her purse and onto the snow.

"Quaaludes no wonder you're so hopped up and disrespectful to me," he hissed.

"Yeah, well these little brown capsules help me sleep during the day. Along with some hard liquor, they act as an antidepressant."

"These pills are illegal, and have no legitimate medical use. Where did you get them? I should haul your little dumb-ass in for drugs and verbal abuse."

"You're beginning to sound a lot like a Narc," JeZe Bella responded in a highly critical tone. "Why are you raising contentious damn questions?"

"I'll say you certainly don't fear the cost of candor." There was a new bitterness in his voice.

"Yes, I know." She was driven by the same unrelenting logic. "And I know you were there the night of the fire in Tony's apartment."

"Nope!" he growled, even as she caught his look away expression in his green eyes.

"As it happens, Lieutenant Bloodworth would like for me to come forth and tell all I know about that crime or whom I might suspect."

"That might prove to be an occupational hazard for someone. I mean, someone could really louse up your beautiful face for telling big fat lies."

"Stop your bullshit, you don't scare me. I'd like to see you hang for what you did to Tony Savage and spoiling my big career."

"Shut up. JeZe Bella! Who do you think would believe you now? Besides, everyone knows my wife, she is a real saint," he smirked. "Annie would do anything to protect my two sons, even lie for yours truly. So, think on that."

Relentlessly, the icy wind whipped at her back. The weather had turned colder and disagreeable. She saw a flush of color on Barry's cheeks, a kind of hectic redness. Looking out in the distance, proving the bad life was good, the prostitutes walk by under the neon lights, letting their customers' gaze drift over them. With thousand-dollar brassy looks, the girls strode their stuff on the sidewalk, only to latch on tight when they were given the big money pitch.

"I despise the street tricks, all of them," Barry sneered. "Shit, at the silly bastards offering up their hard-eared money."

"What's the difference, Barry? These day's all the girls get banged, money or no money."

"That certainly describes you all right. You're just the little whore to prove your own point." Unable to restrain himself any longer, he wanted to hit her but ruthlessly grabbed her arm and yanked like a ragdoll.

Jeze Bella felt that she was doomed, utterly doomed. "Let go of me, your crazy prick!" she screamed rigorously. (Be careful, JeZe Bella!) Those few but precious words echoed the warning bell in her head over and over, as if Tony were saying it still. When, she broke free of his deadly grip, and his febrile twisted mind. Pushing him back, he fell backward into the snowy back alley, losing his baton and grip as he stumbled over to pick it up.

As Jeze Bella lunges past him and runs pursued by a thousand nameless fears and one whose name is all too clear.

While she faded into the drifting crowd on the street, Barry zipped up his *warm leather* jacket as he meandered down the city sidewalk, looking for her. Like a western gunfighter, he had acquired that kind of a swaggering walk through a heavy, milling crowd. In a constrained mood, he paused in the doorway of a club. Raking the place with his greenish eyes, he listened and watched. Bleary-eyed from the late hour, the club's owner nodded his head. Barry turned away slowly, moving down the sidewalk with an almost imperceptible roll of his broad shoulders. He knew the first rule of the street was not to show fear, for this would only act as a goad. Caught in the throes of his violent nature, he was sickened at the very sight of these young corrosive courtesans who infect the street corners. Drifting back into a psychosis, Barry felt the warm sweat soak through his clothes. Silently, he stood tall, lean and totally confident. Operating with great speed, precision and cat like balance, he ran along a flight of His steps. His eyes were the of a tiger, focused to a sharp point a few steps beyond, where an unsuspecting lone female stood under a window. Precipitously, the demonic brought on a street killing. The young woman with long black hair threw up her hands and begged for mercy, only to be stabbed and butchered to death, left dying on a bed of fresh snow. A silver stiletto switch blade was firmly implanted in her back. Gruesomely, the evidence had been left behind to gleam in the moonlight. There was a Black Panther caricature engraved into its steel handle.

Emotionally, across the way, witnesses cried out at a score of policemen who immediately sealed off the area.

"Cherokee Bell wouldn't have hurt a fly. Why her?" a girlfriend asked, extremely skeptical.

"It was a damn cop who did this. It isn't enough they steal our dough but do they have to kill us too?" another girl reflected.

In the spectrum of human responses to this horror, the investigating lieutenant tried to remain objective. He understood the kind of pressure the police force was enduring each day now.

"Sergeant Harris, here's the kicker," the Lieutenant started to say. "We have a duty to ourselves to find and stop this bad cop before we end up with another Jack the Ripper on our hands."

"No cop should wear a badge who acts like this toward people in general," a news reporter screamed.

Amid this ghastly moral outrage, a young, angry woman lamented, "I feel sick to my stomach every time I see a cop's face."

"Lieutenant Bloodworth, I'd like nothing better than to smack that slut's mouth shut," Sergeant Harris remarked over the hostile reception of the growing crowd of onlookers.

"Ease up, Harris!" the Lieutenant's eyes looked narrow and hard. "I know there is a lot of frustration here. You guys have all these pent-up emotions of hostility. And then when something like this occurs, it comes straight out. Well, we have to learn to be more realistic and use self-control because the public is starting to see us cynical."

In the wake of the murdered prostitute, her fancy cohorts roamed the hustling boulevard in quite confusion, like and endangered species, even as the confident pimps sat inside their luxury automobiles surveying the action with an overwhelming support of bail money. Throughout the nights that followed, everything was sharply contrasted because of the local disorder. More bad weather drifting over the snow drenched city, while the police department worried about its collective image amid the stir of a new bribery scandal connected to prostitution and organized crime. The most venomous news columnists were saying publicly that the police of N.Y.C. couldn't sink much lower. Flabbergasted, the ethics committee announced plans to investigate, to see how many police officers were actually engaging in improper conduct, which at worst could lead to their suspension from the department. These very maligning rumors and investigations rock throughout the law enforcement department and the correction agencies. It was a most traumatic time for both the men in blue who wore badges and those who valued the law institutions' reputation. Publicly, some law officials were on the offensive against the newspapers, TV media and internet, saying it was criminal the way they were being dragged through the muck and questioned on how the FBI chose them as targets for a sting investigation. It was a case made potent by the election year and politicians trying to take the heat off them. Meanwhile, the governor called the slaying by an officer on the force, "An act of unconscionable violence which should be met with swift action."

THE HEAT IS ON

CHAPTER 21

Soon another heartless night took on the trademarks of an insurgent campaign against the sleek beauties, with the police on the defensive. They called it new order and were now screening the male clientele that entered the motel-hotel circuit by the airport, as tired old clerks check in the customers in full defiance of the law.

"The chief doesn't have the Mayor's endorsement on this one," Sergeant Romero said to his partner, Amboy, inside the black and white Police van that slowly lanced by the business area like centurion guards of old Rome. above

High in the dark, starry sky, jumbo Jetliners screeched New York City, heading toward Kennedy International Airport, a gathering place for the lacquer-face, high stepping female degree who exhibited the reflection of an avant-garde business. They appealed to a clientele of well-bred executives with smooth manners and plenty of money who flew in from all parts of the country, and Europe seeking new business for their firm while taking the time to indulge and gratify their own lurid desires. But since the new ordinance and crackdown on the city's prostitution, the most enticing among them still loomed out in the lobby of the airport's rent-a-car stands, risking the possibility of meeting head-on with the undercover vice squad.

In the gleeful moment, a pipe bomb went off with a highly explosive force that rocked through the entire building. Could this be Islamic

Terrorism? Miraculously, no one was hurt. Trapped in the chaos, a jetliner soon had to be evacuated of its two hundred forty-eight passengers. Authorities were made to act on a hot tip that a second more powerful bomb was aboard the Boeing 727 Flight 309 to France. Snarled abruptly in the disorder, a police force arrived on the scene to help evacuate several hundred panic-stricken people from the Pan American World Airways terminal.

"Officer Brent!" JeZe Bella looked up, noticeably surprised.

"Well, if it isn't JeZe Bella," he said, looking down his nose at her.

"You'd do well to know you won't get an admission out of me." She had a soft, intent way of speaking; it was enough to charm a cobra.

"It's true then," he remarked drily.

"Are you really so callousing as to ask me that? Look, is Barry here too?" she asked, in the super-charged atmosphere.

"If I, was you, and I'm glad I'm not, I wouldn't be waiting to find out." His anger had managed to spill over as the newsmen appeared with their mini-cams.

Nervously, JeZe Bella turned away from the noise and confusion of the crowd.

"Officer Barrett! Don't make me tear your head off." Police Chief Abraham fumed. "Get those people moving? I've got half the precinct men and the bomb squad here on this emergency. Still, I can't clear this damned facility."

In the prompt action rushing past them, the bomb squad searched the airport's premises, using trained German shepherd dogs to sniff for explosives. Aghast at the situation, the FBI agents tried to keep the circumstance at hand under control. The word was that a man bearing a heavy Arab accent had phoned the airport authorities, saying he represented a home-grown Islamic resistance group. This was the same group who claimed responsibility for the pipe bombs that exploded in a number of lockers at Manhattan's Pennsylvania Station on December 21st.

Besieged by the terrifying terrorism headlines stories that consumed the daily news anchors, JeZe Bella knew she couldn't go back out into the perils of the street with Barry Stark hot on the scent. Buying time, she remembered a magazine tabloid called Screw that she had glanced through at a fashionable hair salon on Lexington Avenue. The tabloid advertised an escort service, a front for career girls who moonlighted as part-time party-girls to make ends meet. Impetuously, JeZe Bella picked up the cell phone and entered the faint numbers still in her mind.

"Hello, Cosmopolitan Escort Service," a woman's voice answered.

"Hi, my name is JeZe Bella," she said calmly. "I'm looking for work."

"Are you over eighteen? And do you have a husband or boyfriend?"

"Yes, to the first question, and no to the other two."

"I run a ligament enterprise whatever you do?" the woman said with a devilish laugh.

"If the money is good, I can play the game."

"You certainly are up front about it. And now I must tell you, whether you're young or highly experienced, we take a large percent of the profit because the men are our clients. If you are still interested, you will work a time schedule that I stipulate." propose I can start?"

Disgruntled, Jeze Bella asked, "When do you propose I can start?"

"Tonight, you may consider yourself gainfully employed by our service. Oh, and by the way, we like it if you can work around the clock. You'll meet the clients at their destination or even at their private addresses. The majority of our clients are married businessmen or professional types. Above all, their names must be kept confidential."

With the descent of darkness, symbolically the grounds' mist rolled away from a low snow-capped wooded hill. Glimpsing the façade of a Kremlin-like mansion, JeZe Bella alighted from a taxi in front of two large white scrolled doors. Robbed of her imaginative powers, she walked in unannounced.

"Hello! Hello!" Amid the dramatic beat of her heart, her own voice resounded from every corner, and with the strangest sensation,

JeZe Bella's eyes swept the immense room that amplified her echoing heels like hoofs upon the glistening marble floor. Suspense fully, she was drawn to an ornately large portrait on the wall; it was of a woman who had somehow escaped modernization.

"Do you like it?" a man's voice swiftly asked. "She was a Russian Countess who left Russia during the Bolshevik revolution in 1917. She is dead now. I'm speaking of my great grandmother, of course. I remember that she had arthritis and that it her trouble every time it was going to rain. She claimed she was the best meteorologist around." gave

At the top of the stairs, the man appeared from the shadows into a very dim, dreamy light, wearing a dark silk robe. His hair was white and he had diamond-blue eyes. With a warm look, he lit a cigar. "You get what's going on my dear?"

"In all seriousness, yes," she replied, with a flouncing posture.

"There is something incredibly sensuous about you. Your shining black hair. The way you move and the way your eyes catch the soft chandelier's light. Tell me, sweet thing, are you into SM?"

"I find the subject quite passé." She glanced at her gold watch and then looked toward the doors, her only escape.

"Do you think it is time to go?" he asked. Unexpectedly, his robe opened a bit below his stomach. He was naked underneath, with a full erection, and as soon as he noticed it, he pulled the robe shut, tugging at its long sash tightly.

"Well, if you aren't the lowest. You've got to be at least eighty, pop."
"Come back here! How do you expect to get back into city?"

"Simple, I asked the cab driver to wait for me."

"But I've paid the escort service for you."

"So, call the Better Business Bureau." With that, JeZe Bella slammed out of the place, putting an abrupt end to his zealous pursuit of words.

On returning to the boardinghouse, JeZe Bella discovered she has dropped her keys along the way and must ask the manager for a second key.

"You girls are more trouble than your-worth," the frowzy blimp in a housecoat call after her. "I am not in the business of given' out keys in an endless supply."

"Oh, you are making your money ten-fold!" JeZe Bella yells back in a way that draws laughter from behind other closed doors.

"What do you mean, I run a respectable place." Slam!

Peace. Quiet. Safety. A moment away from a woman's raucous voice, a john's groping hands, and Barry's menacing stare. She unfolds the morning paper still lying on a chair, finds herself staring into those same eyes, that same face, and hastily scans the front-page story. To the circumstances surrounding Officer Brent Barrett's death are clouded but concern themselves with an offduty party where a mixture of alcohol and firearms have allegedly resulted in the loss of one officer's life.

"We were just clowning around," Barry Stark is quoted as saying.

"He was more than a partner. He was like a younger brother to me."

JeZe Bella remembers her brief encounter with Brent Barrett earlier in the week when a jostling airport crowd threw them together for a few brief words. She remembers the hostile, judgmental look as if he were confirming his worst suspicions about her, which forced her to wonder what if anything, Brent would tell, Barry. Could that incident have had anything to do with this? JeZe Bella cradles her head in her hands and tries to think as Barry would. But still the story read, Officer Charge in Slaying of Fellow Cycle Patrolman, read the morning headlines. The Associated Press went on to say in an article of their own that a 31-year-old New York City policeman accused of shooting and killing his partner at an off-duty party in Central Park was charged with aggravated manslaughter.

Officer Barry Joseph Stark was arrested after the shooting incident, the authorities said. The five-and-a-half-year employee of the city precinct police force was arraigned before Superior Court Judge Alfred DuVal and was being held in lieu of $50,000 bail. Cycle patrolman, Brent Barrett, Jr., age 29, had been shot during a sequence of events, authorities claimed. A fellow officer stated, "the defendant, Stark, with a .38 caliber revolver in his right hand, pointed at the head of the victim with the hammer cocked."

"If I had to make an educated guess," a high-ranking official interjected in the brief news conference, "I'd say it might have been horseplay that precipitated the shooting incident."

"I heard the fight began after officer Barrett grabbed Stark's clipboard and threw it to the grass." The reporter hurled the accusation with a shake of his head. "Then too, I heard that both men had been drinking heavily and became abusive and combative that night."

"There were strong indications that it must have been a good drunken party. Our tempers have flared and simmered here today over the gossip that has run rampant in all directions. But I will say that alcohol and guns don't mix. And this is the tragic result of clowning around," he said, noting that he knew of no indication of anger before the shooting took place. On this date, police authorities admitted that there were about three dozen police officers at that after-hours party in Central Park, but four other precincts attended the same rowdy weekly gathering. Also, city precinct Police Chief Abraham denied he acted hastily when he put twelve police officers on furlough for their roles in the off-duty drinking beer party and because harassment of vagrants and transients who sleep in the famous park.

Inside his office, the chief brewed a tea bag in a ceramic mug bearing his name. "This is a hot topic," he said, and chuckled as he stirred the hot tea.

"Currently, chief, you seem confident," Frank March observed, "But I wonder if the facts might have changed if you'd delayed your decision."

"March, you're a good reporter. Look, the facts did not change each time we discussed the matter. If anything, each version of the story got worse. And I'll testify to that during the Civil Service Board of Appeals hearing for the officers in question. Because the strongest evidence available to me was their own statements and judgment in which they admitted attending the brawling party."

"Chief, the extent of the investigation and your quick action have come under fire by Officer Stark's attorneys, the Osgood & Barnes famed law firm."

"They like to turn everything into a personal vendetta."

"More specifically, they claim that you did not have all the necessary information to act on."

"You would think the lawmakers might chime in with praises for good measure, seeing as I'm faced with the people of this city wanting to toughen up penalties and drop all pleas bargaining in exchange for a lesser charge. Yes, Stark has been suspended indefinitely, with pay, until the matter can be resolved. My decision was a difficult one because the man had a good service record and, of course, this suspension will undoubtedly have a devastating effect upon his family."

"But some police officials have recommended that he be fired at once, for violating police rules, the code of ethics, conduct on and off duty, and lack of cooperation with the internal investigation," the reporter replied in an overshadowing tone.

"Well... I'm shocked and surprised to hear this. But the decision on whether the cop will be fired rests with our City Manager, Mark Spence, with a six-member police board of inquiry." The chief was too wise to get trapped by the newsman's phony approach. "I, myself, will withhold my personal judgment for dismissal until the investigation is complete."

RELIEVED FROM DUTY
CHAPTER 22

IT IS NO less than Barry himself is trying to do, while his wife remains tense and isolated by the raw edge of his nerves. He's on paid leave, pending an investigation by Metro NYPD, and suddenly resumes his residence within the fragile framework of a loveless marriage.

"Annie!"

She spun, startled, one hand at her throat.

"I'm sorry, I didn't mean to scare you," Barry said so innocently.

"I was just wondering when lunch would be ready."

It was hard for her to respond as if he were what he pretended.

She swallowed hard. "Is something wrong? You look upset, Barry."

His eyes rose slightly. "I'm tired, Annie. It's been an extremely difficult week for both of us."

"Yes, I'll fix something ... would sandwiches be all right for lunch?"

"No," he sighed. "Isn't there anything else?"

"Yes, I'll heat the leftover pork chops from last night's dinner." In the kitchen, Annie was left standing before a small mound of dishes as Barry trudged back up the stairs. It was past noon; the sunlight streamed through the window but nothing could dispel the mood as he lay on the bed covers in taut silence, with his forehead creased in deepening bewilderment.

Soon Annie had assembled the plates and utensils on the kitchen table. Then she went to call Barry, thinking along the way that there would have to be some changes. She simply would not keep on waiting on him and playing nursemaid as if he were some sort of invalid. Poking her face around the bedroom door, she found Barry's rigid form motionless on the bed. He lay there with eyes closed and his hands folded neatly across his stomach. Suddenly, she had the absurd notion that she was looking at him lying in a casket but then his eyes fluttered open as he reacted to her approaching footsteps.

Back downstairs, Annie hoped to take him by surprise and somehow elicit an inadvertent admission as to the kind of mess he was in. she inhaled deeply, hoping the additional oxygen would stimulate her senses and cause her to think of a way to pry the truth out of him once and for all. She paused in the act of buttering another slice of bread. Barry didn't seem to notice anything odd as he sank back in his chair, already munching through a piece of homemade bread.

"You know something, Annie?" he muttered impatiently as he speared the last crumb from his plate. "I wish we were a million miles from here."

"Yes," she agreed at once.

"If only there were money enough, I mean. Not that this is actually a bad place for the boys to grow up in."

If he was guilty of anything, it certainly didn't show on his handsome face. He stared at his wife, slightly puzzled. "Annie, is something the matter?'

"Why don't you tell me, Barry? You know more about it than I do. I mean, you can't expect me to think your thoughts to be oppositely engaged." In a feverish state, she took his dish to the sink.

He squinted at her curiously. "Look, kindly tell me exactly what's eating you."

"At this juncture, is that really necessary?" Annie countered as he speculated about how much she already knew.

"Well now, I'm not sure how I'm supposed to answer that. After all, you've got precious little to go on except for your own gut feelings."

There is a wall of silence between them that must be penetrated in a way Annie has never previously considered. But now is a time for desperate acts, and in her own desperate way, she finally manages to battle her way through to him.

"It isn't Brent at all, is it?" she asks, in a strange, voice.

"What?"

"This thing that's got you locked away... from me, the children, the world." She pivoted on her heels like a caged lioness.

"Of course, it's Brent and the suspension too. God, all those years on the force, you think they don't count?"

"What really counts for you, Barry? Please tell me?"

"After six years of our marriage, you ask that question!"

"Yes, I've got to ask myself who you are. What makes you happy, it obviously isn't me."

"You can go by all the jealous rumors you hear from other cop's wives. Who would like to get into my pants, don't you see their all envious cunts. I would never dare give them the time of day much less one night!"

"Yes, but they've always served me extremely well in moments such as these. Oh God," she said, with a sudden grimace of pain, "How could you be so completely screwed over this young model? What is it about her, Barry?"

"You sicken me to my very core. But you must intrude upon my personal and altogether selfish reasons-she makes my head spin, puts me on cloud nine and has me doing dog flips too. Is that what you wanted to hear, Annie?" his response to her jealousy revealed quite a bit about his previously unstated feelings about JeZe Bella Reyes.

"You have a semi-automatic for a heart," Annie responded after a moment's hesitation. "Furthermore, I believe the Osgood and Barnes law firm is a conduit through which you got this $50,000 bail money. I wouldn't be surprised to learn that there will be a police cover-up involved in all this."

He seemed totally impervious to her, cold as ice. His face turned chalk white and a horrible fear overtook Annie as she studied him more closely. "Face it, Barry, you're a very sick man," she said at last.

"You have this phobia to be exact, and I've put up with it for a very long time. Please try and understand that your sons are four and five. What do I say when they ask me things? I really don't know what I would have done if mom and dad hadn't consented to take them for the week end. Oh, why couldn't you have listened to my warnings that drinking would eventually lead you to no good? Now you've shot and killed your best friend over some careless words spoken over a street tramp. But with my help, you might still manage to get yourself acquitted on the basis of temporary insanity."

"I'm going out- "

"To see her?" there is a sudden, uncontrollable whirl of his body that tells her she is right. "I'd hoped it was over between you." She says in a low, dismal tone.

"You don't know what you're talking about!"

"That no good hooker, JeZe Bella Reyes!"

"I'm not staying here to listen to this crazy talk!"

"Barry, don't leave!" as she attempts to restrain him, he throws her off and sends her sprawling.

Yes, Barry had all the symptoms of psychotic illness. Revenge burned hotly on his mind, manifested by the flat effect of his intense inner turmoil as he realized more keenly than ever what he must do. Feeling a deadly repulsion, his eyes showed the cynicism of his profession, and the caustic twist to his mouth only accentuated it.

"Annie, you are to blame for all the trouble I'm in right now. You wouldn't have needed to ask me all those questions about this model or Brent's death if you'd been a little more honest."

For a moment his words didn't penetrate deeply enough for her to react. But when she finally grasped his meaning, she was overcome with a severe chill.

"Here you are, thinking you're so much better than anyone else," Barry sneered. "But all this time, you've been keeping a secret from me. Well when I finally found out you were four-and-a-half months pregnant, something everyone else seemed to know already, I listened as my dear friend Brent broke the news to me and then I broke down and cried. This pregnancy seemed like and intolerable threat that you would hold against my freedom. The shock of it all is my only explanation for the events of that night. I contemplated suicide right then and there. I pulled out my gun and proceeded to aim it at my aching head. When, Brent jumped in and tried to wrestle the gun away. It discharged in my hand the bullet hitting him instead."

"Oh, so that's the way you're going to tell it, using me as an ironclad excuse!" Annie spats angrily. "Well, maybe if you hadn't been running around with that woman, I wouldn't have had to hold the truth back from you."

"To hell with what you think!" Barry retorted in the heat of anger, after telling her the circumstances surrounding the entire incident. "I hate you so much; I wish you'd been the one to die." As the curse slipped from his lips, she saw that his sallow face was now mottled with rage, and in the way his words seemed to devour her, she shrank back in total fear.

Annie cries out in panic and anguish, a protective cry that slowly fades into a whimper. "Oh' God, the baby!" She moans, and falls onto the sofa. "Nothing must happen to the baby; she is not the blame."

"Yeah, that little piece of news I picked up from Brent who picked it up from his silly, stupid wife. Made me feel kind of left out of things to have to hear it like that."

"But, I was going to tell you..."

"When, after she was born and named?"

"No, but you had been so distant, toward me."

"So you and that witch had a phone conversation and tried to figure out the best way to tell me something that nobody had a right to hear before I did anyway. Well, that's not the way it's done, I have my pride. And don't you ever mention the name of JeZe Bella Reyes to me again. When it comes to keeping secrets, lady, you're the expert around here."

"I see everything is now out in the open, maybe we can still work something out. There are plenty of other couples who have."

Barry crosses the room and jerks her roughly to her feet. "Okay, you want to talk? Let's go for a ride."

"Well, let me get my coat..." she dreaded.

Barry moves quickly toward a hall closet and snatches the first article of clothing he sees. It's an old hunting jacket of his, and he slings it at Annie as he pushes her roughly toward the door. She is scared and protesting loudly, which only increases his intense anger, causing him to slap her smartly across the face as he drags her down the walk. He shoves her into the black SUV, from the driver's side and pulls madly away from the street curb before she has a chance to unlock the passenger's door. By now she is screaming wildly and the car swerves erratically as he continues to struggle with her and pummel her with his fist. Blaming her for everything bad, that has ever happen to him in his life. And she is the only thing standing in his way for some happiness and a little sunshine.

ON THE RUN
CHAPTER 23

THE VERY NEXT day, late in the dissipating morning, outside a building slum, there was mass confusion as a woman's bloody body was completely shrouded by an army green blanket and then was loaded into a waiting coroner's ambulance. There were repeated comments in the air about the possibility of suicide. The woman had been found dead in her own vehicle. The police report said she had been shot once through the head with a small revolver that lay on the floor of the black 2010 Ford SUV.

"Let them by!" the police Chief ordered, amid a crush of news media video cameras.

In the upheaval, the body was driven away in a white ambulance under police escort through a hungry throng of some sixty reporters, photojournalist and TV video crews. Knowing the ins and outs, Chief Abraham refused to talk to the local news media gathered about him and other police officials who also chose to remain tight-lipped.

By six o'clock, the news on local networks covered the story with an intensive investigation. "The report from the medical examiner has not yet been released, but there is strong speculation that the woman had been dead for a few hours and her body was still warm when discovered. At the scene, Police Chief Abraham declined an interview and refused to comment on whether the death of Annie Stark was murder or suicide."

They flashed her picture on the television screen while an accomplished anchorwoman read the story to the viewers.

"She came to the Big Apple wanting fame. Technically, Annie Stark was a stage actress, not a very good one but an equity-card carrying one. At one time, she managed some minor roles in a few off-off Broadway plays. Our local law officials are looking for her husband, a prime suspect, who earlier in the week was suspended from the police force, pending the investigation of an accidental shooting involving another police officer."

Later that night, the radio news blared out, "Authorities have identified the man, Barry Stark, age 31 as the same officer who was involved in a shooting accident during an off-hours beer party as the killer of his slain wife. Earlier today, stunned neighbors and friends described the police officer as a quiet yet aggressive National Reserve Marine Vet., from the gulf war. Who apparently suffered periodic flashbacks about his war experiences? Witnesses gave this account: about noon on Saturday, tenant neighbors notified the police department that a man was beating up his wife, and much later, he was seen taking her away in what appeared to be a forceful manner. He pushed an elderly landlady out of his way as he came down the sidewalk, critically injuring the woman. A local news reporter quoted police sergeant Romero as saying, 'Barry Stark was somewhat of a passive guy but would show a certain lack of restraint at times and openly threaten citizens who infringed upon his police authority."

The following day the police were seeking new leads on the whereabouts of one Barry Stark who had been spotted twice near a church where a popular Roman Catholic priest had just been slain. Some parishioners there voiced strong frustration and concern over the death of the parish priest, Father Gifford Bowman. One elderly witness source reported that Father Bowman cried out, "I'm not going to go with you. You'll have to kill me here."

Still another person who said he was in the rectory, told police authorities the sad circumstances that had led up to the priest's death. He also asked not to be identified. "I remember I heard Father Bowman says, "The guilt now lays with you, my son, but, God, reins on the just, and unjust.' The cop then said, 'is it God's will for me to give myself up, Father?' 'Yes, Father had replied.' 'You must let the light of penitence come in, Officer Stark. The cop then replied, 'Will the prayer of confession clear my heart?' 'No!" "Then I don't need your sermon, Father. I have no time left to do any soul-searching.' 'In the haste with a degree of devotion, Father tried to stop him from leaving and a struggle ensued."

"It's too sad that any of this ever happened here at Saint Mark's Cathedral. Perhaps the years will serve us to dull the memory and pain over the terrible loss of Father Bowman. He was so well like," Reverend John Deerfield observed on the tawny brown church steps, amid the almost intangible action of this Monday morning drama where a handful of people gathered around him.

It was getting on toward noon, and overhead, the sky was a deathly grey. Lieutenant Bloodworth had reached Chief Abraham's office just before lunch and caught him at his desk. He looked up in a spiritless fashion and waved him in as he put down the forensic ink pen with an annoyed look behind his bifocals. "I expect you have pertinent information on Stark's latest victim?" he inquired, and lit up a cigar.

"It should be clear to you now."

"Yes, Stark has taken too many steps too far," he said, glancing up from his sheet of paper. "In a city, that is a mirror of Babylon."

"Chief, how can you stay so damned calm?"

"Nuts! It looks like I have to because the rough part has just started. The press will nail my ass down; I'm finished."

"Sure, it will be easy now. One dead priest whose body also bore signs of a fight-bruises on his knuckles, face and elsewhere." The lieutenant continued on with the implication. "The official report of the city coroner will bear me out. The priest died of asphyxiation, due to a police type arm choke hold, a method that has come under fire recently across the nation."

"Well Lieutenant, you didn't have to add a sour note. There have been enough feuds within the force itself, calling loudly for me to resign. Clearly, I'm beside myself. It seems my abrasive style has caused me great problems which will never be resolved admirably in the wake of Officer Stark's actions. They stick to me like an unwanted shadow. Still, it's true I've managed to antagonize many key administrative figures in the department, including yourself. So, without further elaboration, be the first to know that I have here my letter of resignation."

"Uh-uh. Well, I'll say one thing it comes too late to afford any lasting gratification." His face went through a succession of emotions. "Nothing can save Stark's hide now. I want him wasted." With a tingly feeling that was pure hate, the Chief responded, "Be my guest. Shoot him apart."

"On the surface, it doesn't sound very noble. This whole thing has turned into a personal vendetta with every cop on the force." The lieutenant spoke with a sagging moral tone. "But we are all subject to criticism."

"In my short-sightedness, so, this is what prompted a dozen pistol-wielding police officers to surround the area where the young fashion model lives that Stark has been running around with. Strange, they did not find her or him in the floor-to-floor search of the townhouse complex."

"Okay, Abraham. At best, he knows we are alert to him. And he won't feel like exposing himself any further."

"I don't believe he is imperfect but like some of us, a death wish." he may have

"Assuming the problem, Chief? It occurs to me that you're obviously under a considerable strain."

Finally, the tenuous nature of his own position had been brought home with a laconic vengeance. "Perhaps," he said in the litany of worries. "But I'll be viewed as a prior fault when the air has cleared." In the most natural scope of things, the Chief held open a confidential green file. "Read this, Lieutenant, Stark's medical records, from the Vet hospital. They've said hire the Vet; he has served our country. Well, this will bring the government crawling and pleading on its knees what with the news reporters' constant streams of unanswerable inquiries, with a gagging, antiphonal stream of inanities, to be irritating even for the congress."

"This is dreadful!"

"You don't have to look so shocked, Bloodworth. I just thought you should know." He watched the other man's expression carefully, unsure if his reception of the news.

"Do you think it's a dumb idea?" he asked anxiously.

"I won't lie but we need a highly trained psychologist in the psycho-chemical field for a first-rate opinion on chemical gases used in the gulf war and its possible side effects as well as PTSD."

"Then we'll get one." The Chief laughed. "Washington may not be happy with the results."

"Do you have any particular man in mind?"

"Honestly," Abraham said, "I'm not at all prejudiced. Oliver Reed, a Harvard law professor, had done a good deal of research on the damned subject. Lieutenant, it would be criminal if the newspaper people got a hold of it just yet."

"Yes, highly unethical." The Lieutenant added his bit. "It would be just like stepping into shit. There would be no getting rid of the smell."

"Ordinarily, it's been my reaction to sit tight and see what happens. However, my regret will be the news media's intervention on things often makes for worse-not better."

"Yes, with the side effects caused by the toxic gases, Stark could go free."

"And then too, the formal proceedings relating to this could drag on forever."

"Still, I'd like to see Stark dead. And with a little more time, he will be. That's why we won't break this news now, and you won't have to resign. When this is over, everyone will know it wasn't the police department's fault and all will be vindicated."

"He's got to be made?" Abraham questioned.

"Yes, you now seem to be centrally concerned. It was from your desk a few months ago that you hid this ill-fated medical document, if I remember correctly. And you've known longer than I and kept quiet, quite literally. So, a few more. Lousy days won't hurt."

"You should know better. I took the risk-let me explain."

"No, my God, the last thing I'd want to hear is your story."

"I wonder if we could be indicted for withholding something." The Lieutenant was forced to grin at the thought but the Chief did not find the remark any more reassuring than he had intended it to be.

THE KNOCK ON THE DOOR
CHAPTER 24

IN THE DEPRESSIVE darkness of bedlam, once again the deadly evil force trapped inside the body of Barry Stark came to light with breathtaking clarity under the night stars to sustain a city gripped in cold terror. It had caused an eerie chill to run down the spines of its inhabitants who presently, without uncertainties cast willful suspicions on every peace officer on cycle patrol duty.

In search of new prey, like a marauding cycle warrior with unflagging energy, Barry Stark raced out an alley way into the wind and slight traffic on the boulevard. An hour later, in a gloomy hallway, there came a strange knock on the door that shook its hinges.

"What do you want? How did you find me here?"

"How?" he looked at her dully with blood red eyes. "Remember that night on the street? I grabbed hold of your purse. I noticed a key hook onto a plastic card that read; Saratoga Apartments. I presumed that was the address you were working out of."

How very clever of you, Barry and so extremely observant, and sharply alert." She felt like an object idiot. "But then again, if you hadn't murdered Tony Savage, I wouldn't have been out on the street."

"Look, I did you a big favor. He was going to blackmail you. With nude photos, you damn slut."

"Say, I don't remember asking you for help. Barry, this is no innocent fantasy you're involved in," She cringed. "Why, in my mind, your wicked thoughts harm people."

"Well, I don't understand your grousing, JeZe Bella. I'm a man whose love for the law and order make him invincible, like a god maybe. I know no fear whatsoever." His brain gyrated. "I just felt a duty to utterly exterminate all the slimy street traffic that's only free to roam the city because our courts and jails are too overcrowded to put them away." The confession came as no surprise. With a matching mental state, his voice was totally twinge with bitterness that had set his white teeth on edge.

Fragile with fear amid a psychological chill and gripping intensity, JeZe Bella could feel the firm pressure of Barry's left hand on her back as he pulled her close. Commandingly, his virile smell was totally male. Trying to step back, trying not to get too close, she whispered, "Stop! I'm as near to you as I want to be." But he continued to draw her in as he held her at knife point. In the perverted madness, for a few terrorizing moments, her eyes flickered over his luminous badge. Quite suddenly, there was a grueling contest between them. Scared and confused, she was standing face-to-face with death itself; confronting a man she both loved and feared, a man who had altered all her dreams. Indignant, she now suppressed a small laugh at the irony of her ailing situation.

"Shut up, JeZe Bella, or sure as hell, I'll slit your pretty throat wide open," he referenced in a dull whisper, so close that she could feel his lips move. Somehow, it was alarming to feel his warm tart breath on her face. Aghast; her legs went numb as she started to slide down along his hard body.

JeZe Bella threw back her black hair, as if immersed in a long, silent scream. Almighty God! She thought. "Well, go ahead and kill me now," she dared aloud. "What are you waiting for?"

He just stood there, staring at her as though he had taken root, while JeZe Bella put her hands over her face. The sheer curdling shock caused the tears to fall through her fingers.

"JeZe Bella, I did not come here to hurt you," she heard him say. "Lord, I came because I need your help. There is no one I can turn to." Barry's eyes closed wearily as he spoke. His hands gripped the air; it was hard to keep his emotions bottled up inside just as an insurgent pain shot through his temples. "Say, I could really use an aspirin, JeZe Bella," he said then with a dark malignant countenance.

"I haven't any," she told him "Would an Alka-Seltzer do?"

"No!" he shrugged angrily. "It seems that my efforts are frustrated at every turn."

Visibly shaken by his intrusion, JeZe Bella sat on the large ottoman opposite him as he slumped back into the brown club chair and remained immobile. Over a gulf of silence, she was left with ample time to reflect upon the state of her own pardonable pride because she could not ignore his serious contemplation and degrading emotion.

"Listen to me," he said in a seething tone, "I've gone through all kinds of tough hell-first in Iraq and now as a cop. JeZe Bella, I've killed lots. I've even busted up a few people with these black steel tip boots. And worst of all, I've done away with my wife and unborn child. Right now, I don't know of anyone I've killed who deserves to die more than I do."

"Barry, you've reduced the enjoyment of my life to an art. But, the terrible shock of you being killed would kill part of me if not all. Why didn't you tell me everything before?" she asked again. "Oh, why?"

"Because! It would have been a cruel and nasty surprise." In the face of her reliance, he recounted, "I hadn't the courage. I was terrified by how you'd feel if you knew that I was mixed up in the city's largest retribution murder spree."

"Look at me, Barry." She slowly sucked in her breath. "I could easily forgive you anything but not loving me."

"Christ!" he added, "Only a slight miracle could save me now." At this point, he needed someone to assume complete responsibility for his life. In a very still moment, JeZe Bella knelt beside him, pulling his head down to hers and held him tightly as wracking sobs shook his warm body.

"Barry, you've bound to be safe here with me for the time being," she confessed. "Judging by the looks of things, you haven't eaten in some days. I know I have some Italian macaroni and cheese in the refrigerator. And it won't take long to fix a fresh tossed salad."

"If I were really insane, I wonder whether or not I would know it?" He mused, as if to alleviate his own doubts. But the fear proved unnecessary. JeZe Bella was most adept at following the easy path and seeing things through his eyes only. He saw a pleasing and vaguely seductive change in her face. She was wearing something comfortable, a sensuous red satin oriental loungewear toga. Her attire had set the tone. Resting her mandarin rouge cheek against Barry's head, she rocked him gently, and they were both silent for one long, tender moment.

"It's all too ghastly," she said at last. "I keep thinking that if I had done something different, none of this would have happened."

"JeZe Bella, stop. That kind of talk won't do either of us any good. You can't go back and run it all through again. In the end, I'm responsible for my own actions," he said decisively. "Not you."

She was forced to realize that it was all beyond her. "How unfair," she sighed. "Frankly, I'd never dreamed of finding you in such a situation."

"It comes as a great shock to both of us, I guess. In any case, it is futile for you to carry my burden because this all started long before we met."

"I wish I could feel better about it," she retorted sadly.

For the first time, he found it difficult to concentrate. "JeZe Bella, I said I'd never hurt you. Funny-after all, it's not quite like reading a detective novel."

Grudgingly, he added then, "If you want to pick up the cell phone and call the police, I'll not stand in your way."

"For whose benefit, as fraught with danger as the present situation is for me, and in your company, it would also prove embarrassing and require some explanation where the law was concerned. I would prefer to avoid that confrontation, if possible." "Then I suppose it won't hurt you any to give me a little time to rest up."

"Listen Barry, I'm not going to leave matters in this posture. You can stay for as long as you want because I love you so terribly."

"Thanks, JeZe Bella."

Inside the kitchen alcove, JeZe Bella had spiked the coffee with a little anisette to help him relax. Barry was a little hungry and wrung out. He drank two strong cups of coffee on the small balcony. Concerned, JeZe Bella knew that if he left, she would not sleep. Finally, she ordered him to bed. Flipping the light switch off, blanketing the bedroom in still darkness, Barry turned on the TV set and lay for an hour, tossing restlessly in the heat of the room before he finally dozed off. The window had been closed tightly as were the long-flowered draperies. JeZe Bella watched him in the dim light of the luminous TV Screen and listened to the midnight news and the state's most accomplished newscaster. He announced that the police authorities were checking Barry's fingerprints through the F.B.I. he also went on to say that the governor would make the death sentence available for him, making it hard to protest capital punishment. At last, to solidify his point, a TV poll asked viewers if they believed in the death penalty and 2,000 said yes while only 692 said no. It wasn't a scientific poll but it cleared up everyone's doubts. JeZe Bella Carefully leaned over the foot of the bed and turned off the remote control on the TV set.

"I'm sort of popular, yaw know what I mean?" with dark terror darting back for a moment in a confused plea, Barry's voice rang coldly. "The court can set an execution date when I'm caught. I won't beg for my life. I faced that a long time ago. I don't want any pity from anyone when I'm on death row."

"Easy, Barry, a lot of people are pissed off because they're scared." As she spoke, he unbuttoned his pants and pulled them off.

Gently, she touched his hard back, and when he turned toward her, she smiles and said, "Goodnight, Stark."

His mind was tired and craved only the pleasure of sleep. After a moment, the physical and mental exhaustion took its toll of him and he drifted off. That night, death seemed far and not of the present. Once JeZe Bella had undressed and laid down away beside him, she too fell into a deep, lurid sleep and they spent five solemnized hours, warmly oblivious to everything around them.

Early the next morning, Barry awakened from croaking destitute power. He heard the shower running and a crazy, warm feeling rushed over him when JeZe Bella came out of the bathroom, she had a beach towel draped around her like a sarong, and another wound around her head in a turban fashion. The clean smell of sweet soap radiated from her Camay body. When she saw the gun and swooned back against the doorway as he lunged for it over on the nightstand. She looked at him suspiciously. "Barry!" she cried.

He scrutinized her closely. She looked back at him, slightly mocking. "I promise, I won't attack you when your back is turned." He then eyed her with faint amusement. "Do you know, I might like that if you did?"

"I know," she murmured and took his leather jacket and automatically hung it up, together with his pants and shirt.

Barry was completely sober, clad in a T-shirt and sweaty white briefs, about to take a shower. In the light of day, without anticipation, he glanced around the studio type apartment. It was sparsely furnished and scrupulously neat and functional.

"JeZe Bella, don't you ever feel shut in, confined? I mean, living alone."

"It does have its advantages," she replied with a shrug. "When I first came to work in this big city, I shared a place with two other girls. But as little as we were there, we still managed to get in each other's way."

The situation was beginning to look more alluring to her. As she strode across the room and settle down on the bed in a position that afforded a good view, she leaned back in a relaxed manner and waited. At first, it appeared that Barry might defer this opportunity with her, but as the silence lengthened, he favored her with one of his more magnetic smiles and the implication was plain.

Languidly, Barry's eyes looked into hers as his right hand moved warmly up her knees. Without a pause, JeZe Bella bared her firm breast.

"Oh, you cheat, you knew?" she poked in gentle fun.

"Naturally," he said, with admirable foresight.

"Barry, I'm afraid you're just too willing to take advantage of me."

"Strange that you should use those very words, however, m'dear, I did have something of the sort in mind."

"Stop teasing me this way," she entreated. "Be a little sensible."

"But JeZe Bella-you know you have only yourself to blame." His back arched menacingly as he spoke.

"Alas, you've caught me in a sweet lie. I confess-I planned this moment last night, and again when the first light of dawn found us still cling to one another. I hope you're satisfied.

"Yes, last night, I too made a few desperate attempts to push back the sheets that stifled me. But every little movement became exhausting. My mental powers seemed totally numbed; thinking and become an effort, and so I conceded then you did not exchange a single word I muttered."

"Barry, which one of us would have had the energy to make love? Although our minds were quite able to envision all the necessary movements, neither of us could have managed the actual physical act."

"It couldn't be helped, JeZe Bella. We just had to do without. It was extremely difficult for me just to go get my boots off. It was like struggling in quicksand."

"It's rather disturbing-and sad, you alone in your world, and I alone in mine. But perhaps together we can overcome our tremendous pain."

Barry took her face in his hands and forced her to look at him. "Afraid, JeZe Bella, why, I'm not going to do anything you wouldn't want me to do. I promise."

"I'm not entirely sure of that, Barry."

"Don't worry, because, I'm sure." He kissed her in his strong, amorous way. "That should more than satisfy you!"

"Oh, Yes!"

In this moment of unrestrained tenderness, they pursued their mutual physical attraction to the steamiest heights. With a longing flicker in her dark eyes, she embraced him ardently and allowed herself to be swept away on the hot waves of sensual emotion.

HIDING IN PLAIN SIGHT
CHAPTER 25

THE DAY WAS cold wet, but inside the comfortable room, curtains were tightly as the fire burned brightly from within the fireplace.

Stroke-by stroke his dark hair was bleached out blonde and buzzcut away. Finally, he paused as something moved in his intellect; his overall behavior was disquieting. In the soft light, before a mirror Barry emanated a sophisticated Park Avenue appearance. This was due, in no small part, to JeZe Bella's dubious undertakings. For the moment, she too was living her own private dream, rather than face the possibility that the end might be near for both of them.

"Barry, you're so tall and very handsome, and have such good form!" she said admiringly. "I expect you inherited that from your father."

"So I've been told." His utter calmness was alarming. "But at the moment, I'm annoyed with myself."

"Why?" she queried. "It's all very odd."

"Of course," he responded. "And so is my mood. At any rate, the dark grey suit fits perfectly. JeZe Bella, you shouldn't have squandered your money on me this way."

"That' may be the way you look at it, but the fact is, I was sick and tired of seeing you sprawled about in that uniform of yours. It looked dreadfully uncomfortable, but the only alternative was simply out of the question. It would never do to have you walking around the apartment naked all day."

"No... that would be a little too disconcerting, wouldn't it?" Barry winked, observing with a coy smile. "Even so, nothing's changed. I'm still the same old Barry underneath all these outward improvements."

"How commendable of you to say so," JeZe Bella responded drily. "At any rate, I hope you won't underestimate the nature of my good deed."

"I must say, you seem to enjoy doing this sort of thing. Tell me, JeZe Bella, am I still a balm to your ego?" he asked, gazing back into the vast mirror embedded in a gold rococo panel off the far wall.

"Yes...and what's more, you're well aware of it," she said, as she reclined gracefully on the comfortable sofa across the room.

Glancing at his watch, Barry suggests, "How about dinner and a late movie?"

"What a perfectly delightful idea! But don't you think it would be a bit dangerous for you to be seen out in public?"

Barry raised one eyebrow quizzical. "I suppose," he said. "But then again, I can't stay cooped up forever."

"I suppose not,"JeZe Bella said brightly and seized her fur coat and purse.

They left the apartment on a wave of laughter and stepped out into the cool crisp air. Enveloped in the sensational sweep of the city, they were a striking pair as they moved through the streets, hugging one another tightly, oblivious to all things around them.

On this Friday night, it was "business as usual" inside the Lone Star Cocktail Lounge, where a bunch of smiling customers had dropped in for a beer as they listened to Dolly Parton sing "Coca-Cola Cowboy" on the jukebox. Across the mirror of the back bar were the logos of various domestic beers, as Barry and JeZe Bella entered, it struck them simultaneously that the place was more of a bar restaurant. A cramped double row of booths, cheaply constructed of walnut-stained plywood, lined the walls. They were all occupied except for one of the end booths, where Barry and JeZe Bella promptly seated themselves. The waitress attending them was short and stocky; she looked as if she could handle anything.

In the endlessly trembling tension of the room, they drank them

Bloody Mary and ate a palatable steak sandwich.

"This is just like Friends on the TV," Barry remarked. "It's a comfortable joint where you don't have to worry about being jumped or anything like that."

"It's a real cozy, quite friendly place-but I imagine it gets pretty rowdy at times."

Barry sat nursing his third drink as a small group of men entered the place. He scarcely noticed them until they passed by and one of them said, "Hey, get a load of the hot broad!"

"Aw, leave it alone," another member of the trio said, and urged his friend over to the bar.

"You really have a way of getting under a guy's skin," Barry murmured with a quick wink.

"Don't give it a second thought," JeZe Bella retaliated quickly. "It doesn't mean anything."

"You must have an option for every man that comes along."

"Look, I can't control other men's eyes or their thoughts."

"That's true-but then again, maybe you encourage it."

"You're not being fair," JeZe Bella hated scenes and had a feeling that one might be developing. "Why don't we go?' she added, and quickly snatched up her coat and purse.

"What's the hurry, let's finish our drinks first." As he spoke, he signaled to the waitress to bring them their checks.

One of the men at the bar was chewing tobacco and staring at them.

There was a long moment of silence as Barry paid the check, then JeZe Bella began to move toward the door, employing the soft, sultry sway of her hips. What with her thick black hair and wide set eyes, she drew immediate attention, much as a smoldering fire would.

"Barry, come on!" she was saying, and after a moment he moved to follow her toward the glass door.

"Sure thing," Barry retorted, allowing his gaze to travel over the three men who were grinning lewdly at JeZe Bella. Once they had passed through the doors, he added through gritted teeth, "I ought to go back in there and pound some sense into every one of those guys."

Back in Jeze Bella's apartment that night, he argued with her until three in the morning. He wasn't so much drunk as he was hangover, and before the argument had ended, a number of items had been thrown about and broken as evidence of the couple's volatile relationship.

The morning after, Barry plucked a pack of Marlboro's from his shirt pocket and jammed a cigarette into his mouth. "I wonder if you've had enough of my temper tantrums." He mused in a sullen tone.

"Look, I'm okay," she snapped.

"Did I talk a lot last night?"

"Enough, Barry, and maybe more than enough." "Look -"

"Forget it Barry. You've got things back in their proper perspective now."

"Maybe, still, I'm sometimes a little surprised to find that things haven't altered between us, after all the things I've said, and done to you."

"Well, it's obvious that you're not happy with me. Why don't we just call it quits right now?"

"Don't say crazy things. Sometimes I get the idea that you don't have the guts to fight back, that's all."

She ignored him, staring out the window into the 8:00 a.m. traffic, and sipping a hot, bitter cup of coffee.

Diabolically, and without a word of warning, Barry slapped his wickedly icy Smith and Wesson revolver into her still warm palm. As she clutched it instinctively, he gave her a fiendish grin and said, "Kill me! Go ahead. Do it! You know I deserve it. No one will prosecute you for doing it."

"That would be a way out for you, Stark," she said coolly. "But not for me."

JeZe Bella did not know what to think of their conflict. She had not given up, but could no longer think of what to do.

Gradually, his mind was losing its grip-there was a scent of resin. "Why should I struggle, JeZe Bella? My body has no feeling left. I'm as cold as marble."

"Barry, this can't be our finish not like this in the eyes of the world." She cried.

"I can't believe it JeZe Bella, I'm so hot for you and you are so hot for me still."

"I guess we both are playing with dynamite."

"Just the way we kiss each other is what makes us so explosive together."

"Yes, Barry. Just like TNT and that's as it should be no matter what happens."

SAINT PATRICK'S DAY

CHAPTER 26

IT SEEMED AS if something were clutching at their hearts, drawing them closer, irrevocably closer to one another and to some dreadful end.

Barry's finger pointed. "What luck? It's the 17th." They hadn't a moment to hesitate, even as they sought to calm their racing hearts. It was late winter, March and the Saint Patrick's Day celebration was underway. In jovial spirits, the city was crowded with hoards of people. Barry and JeZe Bella were caught up instantly in the midst of the grand Irish parade. It was at once an inviting and bewildering sight, a healthy dose of cheap thrills-simplistic narration and marching musical scores thundered damnably loud as hour-long lines waited obligingly to see the spectacular events unfold before their foraging eyes. Invariably, the crowed started to clap to a field of 76 trombones that blared from a Marine band approaching from a distance. The fulminating music soon washed over their festive mood and the gleeful shrieks of children.

While police officers from around the city lead the big parade. Along Broadway, a bagpipe and drum core clamored loudly behind their steel gleaming motorcycles. That was participating in the annual parade, to honor policeman who had fallen in the line of duty. The event was being sponsored by the NYC Ladies Auxiliary of the Fraternal Order of Police.

Downcast, hustled against the corridor of a large department store, they stood motionless. Barry's thoughts had drifted for a moment as the parade passed by. It was full of faces he knew well, the hard faces of the police force, except for a few softer, more youthful ones.

"Strange, isn't it, JeZe Bella? I was in this same paraded a year ago." He seemed dejected. "A whole year ago, it doesn't seem possible that time could pass so quickly."

Jeze Bella felt sorry at the very mention of it. She watched him lower his eyes, as if searching for a lost memory.

"Oh well, it's all a childish game of politics." He paused again, seeing the helmeted faces before him. "One is willing to go through a great many meaningful ceremonies in order to do one's job-wear a uniform and even salute while standing at attention." Barry didn't think of himself as a martyr or a fanatic-he felt only a last, final weakness, the fear of being discovered. For a moment, he almost forgot about JeZe Bella standing beside him. "Funny, I still feel as though I have my creaking boots on." He raised his head and looked once more at the red, white and blue wave in the air and then turned toward JeZe Bella for some measure of assurance. Immediately, a feeling of compassion surged up inside her; she could well imagine * his sorrowful curiosity, and knew that despite his bitterness, he had always loved his job and country. *For the moment JeZe Bella would not be a kill joy. Her regal beauty kept admirers at a distance. She vowed she'd never marry - there were to many cold-hearted bastards in this world today but she had fallen for Barry hard. Now with an iron fist she put her new troubled past behind her. She had no dynasty to live up to like a strange saga or a tale of some traitor coming to a fine end. Yes! For now, there was no remorse to be had everyone dies sometimes. But had Jeze Bella sold her soul to a man that had no soul left of his own?*

MAGICAL THINKING
CHAPTER 27

ONE CHILL MORNING as the week unfolded, there was a new snowfall and the city was once again stripped of its local color. It was 9:30 a.m. in upstate New York at the grand New England-style estate home of Oliver Reed. Sitting inside his small personal library was Chief Abraham, who was sharing a cup of coffee with the noted law professor.

"So, tell me, Abraham," Oliver Reed said, "How do you see your future these days?"

"I've hardly had time to think about it," Abraham admitted. "At any rate, let's get back to the matter at hand. And I'd appreciate the truth, Professor."

"I'll give it to you straight, Chief. I am angered beyond words after reading this atrocious medical report. True, the statistical information doesn't lie in this type of case-where there is behavior modification. As when someone upset Barry Stark, he wished them dead. Psychoanalysts call it 'magical thinking'."

"The whole thing gives me bad vibes."

"Still...the story should be told. The whole truth, with no holds barred. You should not be concerned about any reprisals, chief," the professor stated flatly. "Think of all the Barry Starks who are sadly dying a very slow and painful death due to exposure to all sorts of chemicals gases like defoliants used in the Vietnam War and who knows about the gulf war we've are still involved in."

"You make a damned convincing argument," Abraham said aloud, although he seemed highly perturbed by this strong suggestion. "But Barry Stark is a deadly apparition now. He could turn against any one of us in the blink of an eye. Besides, we are no longer dealing with a rational police force, but one that possesses a search-and-destroy instinct toward him."

"My only feelings of outrage concern themselves with the fact that he was a most formidable foe of this deadly terrorist Islamic warfare that might have dehumanized him. How many more like him are out there, do you suppose? Once these chemical gases are absorbed through the skin tissue and enter the blood-stream, it attacks the nervous system, the mind and eventually turns a man into a monster."

"So that's why the thought of committing a crime didn't worry this guy or even the thought of deliberately hurting someone," Abraham mused.

"Yes, I daresay it would be enough to look into this man's eyes to get a real glimpse of what hell is all about." Oliver Reed pondered the idea.

"I'm no bleeding heart, professor. But I'm with you," the Chief said. "It's altogether possible that the department made errors despite my best efforts to prevent them. You see the New York Department of Public Safety records revealed no connecting threads among this tapestry of murders. In the span of bloody carnage that sweep through so many precincts, there was no reason to connect them all to Barry Stark, except for Lieutenant Bloodworth's hunch which I was inclined to dismiss quite instinctively."

"I guess the truth is much more than just looking into a mirror. We sometimes have to feel inside ourselves."

"Look, Professor. You have to kick hard enough in this world in order to be entitled to kick back."

"I hope you've got the guts."

"And what am I to make of this girl, JeZe Bella?" Abraham wondered aloud. "A New York Cover-Girl, up-and-coming model, who took up with Stark."? He asked the question in a joshing way, as if to cover up his ruminated emotions.

"Well.... Her motive for throwing herself so hastily into a dangerous and disastrous affair was certainly not motivated by sympathy. It's my guess that she was governed by strong feelings of self-hatred." He recollected. 1

"It's all about Social Conditioning, would you say?"

"Yes, Chief, Varying degrees of guilt and depression, it is a stereotypical form of logic." The Professor's glasses slid part way down his nose as he stood and walked over to the fireplace. His hands were jammed inside his trouser pockets. He tried to speak normally but his voice was strained and tense. "I have something I must tell you, Chief Abraham. Please, you must trust me. I am speaking to you as a true colleague. Believe me when I say there is no need for secrecy where this medical report is concerned. It is like an omen that you came here with it today, because tomorrow, on Good Friday, I was to speak out at an outdoor symposium in Central Park on the behavior of our nation's Vets. This is why the VA administrators must stop dragging their feet, and start helping these soldiers."

"Technically speaking then, my decision to turn over Stark's file to you might attract attention to these forgotten men."

"Indeed so. Barry Stark will be but an echo for all the voices of those poor unfortunates, and most probably, he will be an influencing factor in getting the Yale Federalist Society, an organization of conservative law students, to assail the high court so that some type of decision can be made in getting help for those thousands of Vets who still have not adjusted back into society due to an immoral war that caused an entire nation to hate their own G.I.s. this is why I feel the young law students and the news media today have the power to influence the judges in the courts of our land. They can do it with their special middle-class values and not the liberal ideas."

"Why would the press respond to Barry Stark now?" the Chief asked a trifle doubtfully.

"Because from the '60s on, the news media has become heavily left liberal and turned our social morality on its ear."

"Professor, you make it sound like they will not sponsor legislation and all because of their distaste for the military and war hawks."

"Well, it's up to the people to nationalize morality. What this man ultimately did, was not of his own choosing, war changes men."

"I'm afraid the constitutional rights of Barry Stark will expand beyond all bounds."

"And why not, chief, a good defense lawyer will contend only the true issue. I trust his mental state and graphic behavior will make it reasonably easy for the jury to consider this case in a fair and equitable manner despite the shocking atrocities."

"I half expect the government to try and block testimony and turn it into a battle of psychiatric experts if not a side show as women faint over this GQ cop."

"Chief, even with Stark's magnetic looks, 50,000 vets can't be done away with so easily-not when Washington is planning to break ground for a national memorial to its vets who now fight the war on world terror. How could the Congress of this country be so indifferent to their long-suffering problems?"

"If I know the Federal Government," Abraham countered, "They will refuse to release any history on the gases used on the first Gulf-War, if only to protect themselves and the Military from any disability litigation brought about by a national outcry."

"Chief, you sound like a lawyer, but still, here we have a means of finally testing the truth strength of the Freedom of Information Act." He gave Abraham a sharp loc and lapsed into a thoughtful silence.

"Overnight, Barry Stark could become a national hero ..." the Chief remarked then.

"Only if you can somehow prevent him from being killed before I've had a chance to speak out publicly on his behalf."

"Perhaps your right professor." There was a kind of conscious mockery in the Chief's voice as he and the professor sat together, drinking their coffee. They silently toasted their cause and themselves, without even a trace of modesty.

THE PROTESTERS
CHAPTER 28

ABOUT 2,500 BUSLOADS of protesters from over 300 towns and cities had arrived earlier in the week for this day's peaceful demonstration rally. The Good Friday Veteran's Committee said 10,000 to 30,000 people would march from the United Nations to the 18-acre Great Lawn at Central Park to get the much-needed attention of those power wielding decision-makers on Capitol Hill. These Vets were protesting for their right to better health care in the nation's Veteran's Hospitals, and for a more equitable cost-of-living increase to their compensation disability benefits.

The National Weather Service had predicted clear skies with temperatures in the mid-50s. Scores of protesters marched past the United Nations and then across town on 42nd to Central Park along Fifth and Seventh Avenues to converge on the park. The police estimated that 15,000 to 35,000 people would attend the 1:00 p.m. rally. Also, the police department had assigned 370 officers. to crowd control with some added volunteer workers filling in as peace-keepers on horseback.

On the radio that morning, the mayor predicted traffic congestion and urged citizens to use the public subway transportation system if they came into town.

At 11:00 a.m., with the noon hour closing in, the mass demonstration in the street included everything from gray-haired grandmothers to toddlers in their strollers brandishing banners and signs that read: "We have come here with a messaged to the White House and Capitol Hill." Still others read: "Where are the jobs for the mentally impaired and handicapped that have served in war?"

Soon a new field of approximately one thousand anti-war veterans joined in from a side street. It was the Task Force, seeking relief for Vietnam Vets exposed to lethal herbicides over forty-five years ago. Many of them shouted, "Where is our missing in action who served in Nam? How can freedom be ours if we can't help those brothers who fought to preserve it today and yesterday's forgotten?"

Nearby, from inside a large street cafe, Barry Stark looked through the huge plate glass window to see the marchers go past. Symbolically, they carried white posters and signs that were sprayed with splashes of fluorescent orange paint as they chanted, "We shall overcome," and "My Country, Sweet Land of Liberty."

Rather in keeping, if a bit old-fashion, JeZe Bella slipped her arm around Barry's breaking in upon his pressing thoughts.

"Look at me, Barry," she urged. "What's wrong? Don't you want me to touch you?"

He had been acting oddly, remaining strangely silent. "Don't be silly," he muttered tensely, and patted her hand in a quick, wooden gesture.

"If you'd rather not talk about it..."

"There's nothing to talk about. It's just those signs the protesters are carrying. You couldn't possibly know how they relate to me."

They were, for all outward appearances, relaxing over a semi-French cocktail lunch. When JeZe Bella glanced about to see if they were attracting any attention, she saw that the place was nearly deserted. The few people that were left were slowly departing to join the rallying crowd outside. JeZe Bella breathed a deep sigh of relief.

"It's nightmarish!" Barry exclaimed suddenly. "In some bizarre way, it's all finally come home to roost. That still haunts the living hell out of me." He sat wallowing in self-pity. "I've been alienated and tormented by the past for so long that any reminder depresses me. I'm sorry, JeZe Bella. I didn't mean to let off steam like this. But right now, I miss my *warm leather* jacket, my security blanket." ahead, Barry. It's all right; feel free to vent your feelings.

"Go You're entitled to spill your guts once in a while. I'm not going to laugh at you. Honestly."

"It's only that I no longer have any targets for my anger-except myself."

"Open up to me, Barry. You don't have to hold back more." any with an expression of love on her face, JeZe Bella extended one long slender arm, embellished at the wrist by a collection of gold bracelets.

"It's so horrible, JeZe Bella. I carried a foreign-made min-Uzi automatic sub-machine gun. The gun fired thirty times with one Short squeeze of the trigger." He cleared his dry throat nervously and then went on. "I've always wanted to tell my story. I wanted to tell my mother but she was dead. I wanted to tell my wife but she wouldn't listen; nor would any of my friends for that matter. I only wanted to feel a little relief about what I had done, but there was no one that would help me out. At night I'd literally gagged and cried in my dreams. It's a very ugly story, JeZe Bella." His head jerked in a curt nod.

"Don't stop now, Barry. It's time to let it out. You mustn't keep it bottled up inside yourself any longer." JeZe Bella squeezed his hand, and with a small smile, urged him to go on.

"Very well, but if it touches you, you'll know why I feel so dirty all the time," he said, recalling the traumatic episode of his young life. "In Fallujah Iraq, I was an artillery forward observer, attached to a Marine infantry unit. Well, one grim hot as hell day out of the Green Zone in Iraq. I found my two closes best friends dead on roadside detail blown up. Under the morning sun, I felt sad and confused. I shook my head to try and develop some semblance of logic for all this. That afternoon, my heart pounded as we set claymore mines all over and around the Saddam Husain's oil fields. The road was a crossing for the militant Iraqi Arab Terrorist who planted roadside improvised explosives devices. Amid the senseless death of my buddies, the ambiguity permeates almost hearing Arabic spoken sounded maddening and I was not a brooding Marine who has returned home after one tour of duty. Emotionally wounded and brutishly diagnosed with post-traumatic stress disorder, to be given prescription drugs without doctor's orders." Barry's view was not grounded in reality or reason.

JeZe Bella suspected some twisting things were going on in his head. Was all this PTSD that had turned him into something of a hit man? Who never escaped his dangerous military past still battling the American's invading an alien country?

Barry Stark rolled up his short sleeve that had shown a large tattoo on his right arm that read "Slug" a nickname his buddies called him for a reason. "I remember clearly a moment of horror as I stepped from behind our Humvee at a cargo truck stop. Alone figure of a tiny woman and small child, appeared on the side of the road carrying a sack over her right shoulder. Well, to make a long story short, I killed both of them, because I hated them all. They all stole from us-all sorts of personal belongings-then sold them on the black market. Killing that woman was a stupid thing but it was my way of getting even. But her horror-stricken brown eyes looking into mine-not theatrically, just pleading her life and child's. Even so, I raised the muzzle of my M-16 rifle and savored the effect it had on this terrified woman. When, a rapid automatic burst from the rifle exploded, and I could still see her anguished, pleading eyes looking at me as bits of her bloody flesh stuck to my combat uniform and face. I can still feel the effects of that scene." He shrugged in a way that told JeZe Bella a lot of things. "Anyway, that hot spring, about eighty of infantry struggled and cursed our way through the Middle Eastern weather wind sand and lots of sweat. And some of us lost our lives there. I know I almost did as I carried my hundred pounds of gear and ammunition that jerk at my shoulder straps. I soon gave up trying to walk for I was slipping and sinking in the sand, stumbling for days in order to rendezvous with the resupply helicopter that meant food, water and mail in that order. None of us had eaten since the day before. It seemed as if the gnawing hunger had chewed its way through my burning stomach. Then it happened: all my thoughts were interrupted by the infuriating sounds of airplanes. It was the U.S. Air Force overhead, spraying bullets in a case of friendly fire on our perimeter. In the midst of this senseless act, for reasons totally unknown to us at the time. We all tried to dig foxholes in the sand to escape the brutality of our circumstances. We waited for a day in absolute silence for some word from a helicopter rescue to help the wounded and hurt. Some of the Marines died there, while others, like me, died only a little. My head throbbed madly and my eyes saw flashes of bright colors. Far in the distance, sounds of another road explosion brought reality back into painfully sharp focus. There were entrenched, snipers firing upon us, and one marine got hit in the back and was bleeding heavily and it was obvious that he was great pain. To this day I don't know if he survived. We then argued briefly over what to do. The Red Cross helicopter had given our position away. These insurgent's heavy automatic weapons erupted from all sides as our company scrambled for cover. Finally, three U.S. Marine helicopter gunships were called in for some back up support. When the gunships made their approach, they flattened out the ground as the fusillade of rockets left the pods on the lead gunship, ripping through the shifting sand hills. These insurgents darted back and disappeared into the ground. Almost immediately, a Red Cross fleet of eight to ten helicopters landed safely from the heavenly sky onto the open road nearby and our company-what was left of it—was ordered aboard. I was put in a Vet hospital for over a year after that. I tried to tell the Vet doctors about my dreams, dreams in which I committed homicide, but they would always interrupt me and say, 'you're home now kid; just try to forget it,' it was an ugly war, fought for the rottenest political reasons, and that's why no one wants to hear about poison gases and friendly fire. Of the eighty men in my company, all died but me. I was the only guy to make it out of the Vet hospital. JeZe Bella, I've heard that the suicide rate among us Vets is higher than for any Americans in general," he said, feeling that same mood of self-destruction. "To many people, the Vet will always be a murderer, never to be looked upon with any kind of pride as the veterans of other wars."

JeZe Bella felt a rush of tears as his penetrating eyes gave her a sharp look and he added yet another bitter comment.

"You'd think the Veteran's Administration would have launched a probe into why we can't get proper medical help and care as our suicides are 22 per day."

"Barry, it would have cost the government untold millions if there were a link between the toxic gases used and the G.I.'s health and mental problems."

"You're right, JeZe Bella. They would only say now that those claims are politically motivated and absolutely false." He recalled, "Surely everyone by now is damn tired of hearing about the Vet Hospitals. More than 50,000 Vets have complained bitterly to the VA of various ailments including skin rashes, headaches, nausea and even cancer. Some Vet's wives also claim birth defects in their children. I suppose I should be deeply grateful for something that I can't attest to. Well, I'm afraid this controversy will go on forever on the contaminants used in the war." His story grew challenging with a difficulty trying to figure who he was anymore. Barry's reasoning was not grounded in reality a victim of his paranoia and all the violence that had finally erupted.

She saw tears in his eyes and put her hand over his shoulder. "Though it must be difficult, Barry, you need to forget all this."

'Yes," he said. "But what's so terrible are the lonely nights. When I wake up and break out into a cold sweat, and being among people who don't care or understand me-people who never really want to." He sighed deeply. "At last, I've told someone about my war experience and how I came home to a Vet hospital. After 22 months of time served in the military, all I have to show is a commendation medal and a number of citations for outstanding performance in a combat zone. Today, I still don't know why I'm different from all those guys on the police force." He picked up his empty water glass, frowned at it and then put it back down.

"I know how you must be feeling. But if we could sort things out, you might find that we have a few thoughts in common." She understood his anger, at the system and the reason why nothing could be done about it.

"It's funny, isn't it, JeZe Bella?" Barry bowed his head and moved his lips tightly. "Our lives are like something straight out of those revolting Soap-Operas."

"Undoubtedly." She looked at him with a degree of great affection.

He turned to her, saw an unexpected sadness on her face and was sentimentally touch by it. "I know now I'd be lost without you now. And that's no lie." Perhaps he hadn't won her over, but at least someone had listened to him without being indignant. He had kept her on the edge with his ability to offer a glimpse of his vulnerability and painful past still inside his head.

As Jeze Bella eyed him with no misgivings, glancing at him, she saw a well-built man of thirty-one with an attractively handsome face, his bleached out blonde hair that looked like a bit of sunshine and well-formed hands and feet. She frowned. It was possible to learn a good deal about such a man in the space of a few moments. But instantly, she banished the thought that had raced through her mind as he gazed at her with the determination to battle on stamped so clearly on his face. This did not wholly surprise her. Actually, she found it difficult to be annoyed with his changing moods because of all he had suffered through. They sat together quietly, sipping their glasses of chilled red wine.

Sequentially, Barry felt ill for a dwindling moment. He tried shutting his greenish, dragon-colored eyes, certain he was about to be sick. Then he opened them slowly, realizing that this made him feel somewhat better.

JeZe Bella had to laugh at his expression. Recovering from the shock of his experience, she let a smile form at the corners of her mouth. "Thank you, Barry," she said, "I'm happy you chose me to talk to about the war in Iraq."

"It wasn't so terribly painful to tell you, JeZe Bella. Not as bad as I'd imagined it would be." JeZe Bella was amused by his discomfort and wondered if the Latin waiter had noticed it. He was a man who appeared to be honest, not icy cold, and seemed to see nothing rude in staring. She glanced at him and he smiled again. She thought it best to ignore the man lest she encourage a boldness that might become somewhat embarrassing. She then powerlessly looked away from him but was aware that he continued to study her every move. Impulsively prompted, JeZe Bella stepped to the veranda rail and stood with her back toward him, gazing out into the street as people wandered aimlessly about. A passing jet could be heard amid scattered noises and deafening quiet. She turned and asked in a jovial voice, "Shall we go, Barry?" her amicable voice nagged at his conscience as she linked her arm through his and he looked into her alluring face.

"I'm with you," he said, moving to her side. Accommodating the sounds of the chancy afternoon, they left as the café's customers before them had, following after the marching protesters 'procession, like a Mardi Gras crowd after a colorful line of slow-moving floats.

It was nearing the end of a nice dinner. "This is an evening I'll remember," JeZe Bella said, tossing her head back. "After such a long day, I'm ready for a good hot bath and some sleep."

There was a bad moon on the rise this particular evening. As the two of them were leaving the dimly light hotel dining room, Maria Torres emerged from the elevator with a male companion in time to see their retreating backs. The sight of JeZe Bella in the company of Barry Stark caused her to tremble. Faintly shocked, Maria kept her head obstinately lowered. And before she was able to shake the effect off by the gentle prodding of her companion, she rushed over to the service desk in the quiet lobby of the Saint Regency Hotel. In odd contrast, Maria could scarcely control her eagerness. She felt she would burst out of her skin at any moment as she picked up the desk phone's receiver and held it to her ear.

"Hello? Operator, get me the police department." For a brief interlude, their comings and goings had been discovered by Maria Torres. Outside, JeZe Bella smiled up at Barry. Tucking her hand around his waist, they shoveled off, with a slow pace, as if just the movement of walking were highly pleasurable. In due reverence, his hair was neatly combed and his new shoes shone as he wore a dark grey, smartly tailored overcoat. In the course of their first meeting, he had looked intimidating in his uniform. Now he was glossy enough to be mistaken for high level executive type or even a redcarpet stopper. As they walked along, passing a small crowd on the corner who was seeking spiritual enlightenment from a religious fanatic who spoke to them from a loud megaphone.

"If only I could believe those words the swamis speak of," Barry said with a snorting laugh. There was a faint odor of liquor about him and she caught the scent of his burgundy breath as he turned in her direction. Their love had not faltered because by now, his mental agony had become hers. He no longer was trenchant as in the past. He was starting to wear down physically. Clutching one another, they shivered in the cold breeze, and roamed down the street like an endangered species. They looked somewhat subtle under all the artificial neon light that illuminated their own human reflections in the glass windows that mirrored the city and its night people. JeZe Bella was so compellingly clad in a white coat and a long flowing red scarf. She was an addiction to Barry from the very start. His ego suddenly reached out, as he pressed his warm lips and tongue to hers, sexually aggressive. The night seemed supercharged and unstoppable. They were caught up in the perils of the street scene, amid the low life on the sidewalks. Still, the ambience of the city's neon blazed on with a sensory delight. Straying down the boulevard, unconsciously JeZe Bella followed Barry with her cosmetic eyes. He hadn't looked at her much during dinner and hadn't even noticed that she had done her hair differently and was wearing a dress that he had never seen before. He had something on his mind that was most obvious.

"Astonishingly enough, JeZe Bella, I remember Brent and I worked the most crime-infested area of this celebrated city. We were totally dependent on one another and both loomed down on some of the most offbeat streets as easy targets. I can recall many instances when he used to tell me to watch my ass. I'd laugh at him and I said, you got to toughen up guy! Like me, buddy." His voice sounded dedicated and compassionate. The memories explained the emotional fatigue that drained him psychologically. Holding her hand, they strolled across the resounding street, where they would wait for a bus, on a stone bench. Sentimentally, JeZe Bella had been stirred to the depths of her being. She had never known such happiness as in these moments-for they were so intense, and yet, so pure of mind.

"It's strange, I know," she said softly, "but yet I know we are as sure of on another as any two people in love."

"JeZe Bella, it's a universal reaction," he said with a laugh, "to feel we know each other so completely."

"Yes," she agreed. "As if we'd both been lifelong friends for years."
"Friends?" he repeated and pulled her to her feet, kissing her lightly amid voiceless passersby.

"Barry, promise me one thing," she insisted happily. "Promise me that you'll always love only me and no one else."

"Absolutely angel, I know now you could never break my heart" he replied, without a moment's hesitation, leaving her with a feeling that was the quintessence of purity in his tortured heart and soul.

Instantaneously, the excitement evaporated; there was a sudden static in the air. Approaching from a distance, they heard a throng of horrid sirens. The psychological atmosphere changes with the mood, Jeze Bella as if she had plunged into something quite abnormal. She had the very strangest and most vivid impressions; unlike anything she had ever known before. There was an unnaturalness of manner in the way Barry saw everything around him. His strong body was still capable of surviving a good deal of ill-treatment at the hands of his captors. Barry's chief nightmare was an endless one of a man hunted by illusions, who expected to be shot on sight. His eyes told her as much, as with a long steady look, he continued to look over his should into the darkness.

"Fuck this police department! They're not going to get my balls in a wringer tonight," he shouted. "Look JeZe Bella, the heat is after me. I have an idea I should leave you now so that no harm will come to you."

"No, I won't listen to a word of that," she retorted with obvious concern in her voice and leaving no misinterpretation of her feelings.

"But I'm about the ugliest encounter one could ever wish for," he reasoned.

"Don't say that, Stark. Come back here!" she caught her breath and gave chase as he began to move away from her in the multidimensional atmosphere.

Barry had been having mental problems for quite some psychological time, and JeZe Bella had no way of knowing how serious his illusionary mind was working. Engulfed in the roar of traffic noise, he spoke just above a whisper, but his voice echoed off the buildings that surrounded them. He was uncomfortable and guessed that were he able to see what lay around the corner, his heart would be in his mouth. There was something in the moment, a threat of disaster. Or was he only imagining things? When they became aware of someone up ahead of them, Barry was breathing hard sweating from nervousness. He could feel a dozen streams of moisture running down his back.

"My Lord, is this possible?" Barry's voice was loud and clear. "Brent is that you? Answer me!" he had a visual experience of sensory perception.

In him, JeZe Bella heard a quaver that sounded strangely like a sob. He opened his eyes he'd closed in torment and stood much as a statue gazing. There was a strange force at work here somewhere in the unknown reaches of his mind.

"Barry. I'm telling you, that Brent is not here with you now. Your friend is dead, but I know if he were alive, he'd truly want to help you."

The thought was worth pondering. "Hell, I would never give him the chance," Barry argued fiercely. "He'll do whatever Chief Abraham tells him to."

"Listen to me," JeZe Bella countered, "My life never had much meaning or purpose. About all I have left are you. Oh please, Barry, don't slip from me now." She began to sob, putting her head on his shoulder. "I know your world is so painful that you'd rather escape from reality."

"I guess you're wiser than I, JeZe Bella."

"Am I?" she wondered uneasily. "Or have I fallen under your spell and only thinking myself wiser?"

Surely if there were anything wrong, JeZe Bella knew it by now.

"No, we can't stay here. That man's coming for me," while the crazy thought kept running through his feverish mind. "I personally suspect Lieutenant Bloodworth has assigned spies to watch me. I'm convinced he has done many things to discredit me and I know why because he hates my guts." He gasped.

"Surely you can't be serious, Barry!" JeZe Bella protested in an incredulous voice.

"Oh, but I am! He is working with the enemy."

In this last but shining hour, they took a journey through the city with no destination in mind, looming along a path of darkness that made it hard to see; yet it was a darkness that Barry welcomes. When they finally emerged onto the sidewalk from the subway, he sensed that they were some distance east.

"Can't we stop to rest a moment?" JeZe Bella asked as she momentarily halted.

"No, we've got to keep going. It can't be helped. We've got to be extremely careful," he warned. For five minutes more he led the way in damnable silence without even the slightest hesitation. The pelting sweat fell from his brow and he felt a salutary dizziness as they lurched back against the cold stone wall. Suddenly, he could hear the deep-throat snarl of the night breeze as it rushed past the building. After a few seconds, the sound was like a fist smashing at his face and there was thin moist mist in the salty air that he now tasted. Looming along a depressive path of darkness made it hard to see, yet Barry welcomed it. When they both emerged onto the sidewalk from the tunnel, he sensed they were some distance east.

"Can't we stop and rest a moment?" JeZe Bella asked, pausing briefly.

"No! There isn't time for that now." For five minutes more, Barry led the way in silence without a halt. The sweat continued to pour from his brow and he lurched back against the cold brick wall.

"Barry, please!" JeZe Bella entreated breathlessly in his psychotic seizure.

"Keep quiet, JeZe Bella, or you'll give our position away." He spoke with a hushed kind of desperation-through clenched teeth. He then grabbed her hand, and they ran, skirting along the building wall, casting large looming shadows, that swiftly altered their grotesque shapes in a kaleidoscope way.

Barry was frozen with fear, hearing gunfire and rocket shelling all around him. At times it seemed distant and muffled, but at times it actually thundered around him. He was beginning to be haunted by voices in his irrational head, and tried everything he could to get away from them as he covered his ears.

JeZe Bella's high heels provided an excruciating pain at this accelerated gait, as they raced past marquee after marquee and were momentarily bathed in the flickering neon brilliance.

Directly ahead, the atmosphere had become anti-climactic. Barry stopped in his tracks, overpowered by the thought that all the faces on the street were staring at him. There was something hostile in the silence of this crowd, something ominous and forbidding. JeZe Bella sensed it too.

With a jerking movement of his head, Barry commenced looking about him and then abruptly said, "Wait!"

"What is it?" Jeze Bella asked trying to make sense of his logic. He flinched, and she watched his shoulders sag. "They know all about me," he said, intuitively somber.

"What are you saying? Who knows? What do they know?"

"They just know, that's all, for hours they've been muttering away in Arabic. These Iraqi's think they've got me fooled but the insurgent rebels."

"You can't believe what you're saying!" JeZe Bella cried out in sadden alarm. "You---You mustn't say things like that, Barry."

"I can even hear them whispering through the walls of this fucking building. They're talking about me all right." He threw her a wry smile and momentarily closed his redden eyes. "Why can't they just leave me alone? I just did what I had to do, I'm a Marine I was taught to kill, and I did my duty. Everyone else did the same."

"Barry, don't crack up on me or you are a little intoxicated from the wine at diner," JeZe Bella begged. "You're starting to have illusions. This is New York City not Baghdad. There's no one speaking in Arabic."

"Oh, but that's where you're so wrong. They're clever that way. They've put up this false front, disguising their stinking village to make it look like a major American town. Oh, yes ... they're very clever people that way."

With an obstinate gesture, JeZe Bella unpleasantly covered her ears. "I won't listen to this!" she insisted. "Your cerebral mind is playing tricks on you."

"Then, don't listen. Just look around you. Look at their dark eyes they even smell like dirty camels. They're afraid I'll expose them, come on, let's get going. We've got to warn my unit before they fall for this trap." He grabbed her firmly by the wrists and hurriedly dragged her along as this feverish spell was wearing off.

JeZe Bella felt a shiver along her spine. She saw that his face was shining with sweat, and that his eyes were rolling as flecks of foam appeared at the corners of his mouth. He was taking long, gasping breaths and had developed a pallid, haunted look. She saw that his face had lost its original handsomeness.

As the relentless sirens screamed in his ears, he found himself wanting to scream back. An instinct for self-preservation fought valiantly against dark feelings of utter hopelessness. "This way or that?" he kept asking himself.

They went along a random course as a patrol car's spinning red light swept the building walls up ahead. Incredibly, in front of the Hotel Drake, he saw the immediate answer to all his problems. A sleek new bright red Corvette had driven up to the main entrance. As a ritzy platinum blonde stepped out and waltzed into the fashionable hotel, he saw that the car was still running, that it had been left for the doorman to watch and valet to attend too. The Long Island license plate bore the name: 4-Slug. It was a sign ... an omen ...a miracle as his mind cleared!

"What perfect timing!" Barry said with the first hint of a smile. "I've always dreamed of a red Corvette JeZe Bella, driving one along the east coast."

Now at her wit's end, JeZe Bella moved as if to edge away from him, but he quickly whipped her around and steered her toward the automobile.

"Get your nice to look at ass inside this car," he muttered tensely. "That's our ticket out of this hell we're in."

"I-I'm frightened," JeZe Bella retaliated through her confusion. She felt the absurd urge to laugh and cry at the same time. "But, Barry, this is grand thief!"

"Trust me," he urged. "I know I flipped out for a moment back there, but I'm all right now, don't just stand there looking beautiful."

Taking rapid and masterful control of the car, he quickly steered it away from the curb. There was a shriek of tires and the voice of someone, maybe the doorman ordering them to stop in their trail of car exhaust fumes.

As Barry hit the low beams, the white-gold lights illuminated the black asphalt street as he moved out easily into the line of flowing traffic. He drove without haste, expertly guiding the Corvette around sharp corners and pot holes, not wanting to upset JeZe Bella any more than was necessary. He sensed in her a true, fanatical devotion and tried to decide how he felt about her sincerity.

"Hell's bells!" he muttered aloud. "It's Good Friday and in a few minutes, every cop in town is going to be looking for this sportscar. The fact that it's bright red shouldn't make it all that hard to find." He tried to maintain a sense of humor but could taste the fear in his mouth. "Well...at least some of those cops are still friends of mine." He stated in a most charming way but without any deep meaning.

"Still, they've got to uphold the law, Barry. Look, there's another way. If we give up ourselves, the testimony of a good psychiatrist would probably get you off as for me I don't care what happens."

"Don't talk crazy, I'm a man with a large bounty on my head! I'm not going to hang around and run the risk of being blown-up and raged like war buddies." His had eyes grown dull green and he no longer seemed sharp enough to cope with the endless perplexities of his life.

"Barry, please believe me—I'm on your side. But we've got to face certain facts. In an hour or so, we may be forced to give ourselves up and I don't want you to die in all this. It wouldn't be fair to either of us now."

"Shut up, JeZe Bella! Giving up isn't part of my makeup' but you're free to go whenever you want. Just say the word; I can drop your panties to the curb."

"I know you mean that," JeZe Bella said with a low sigh. "But hell, I don't have anywhere else to go now. I never have had. Please let me stay with you!"

"God Almighty, JeZe Bella, I'm burning up inside. I haven't been this sick since they had me in the Vet hospital because of that damnable 911, Gulf War. There's no telling what the hell they've done to me with their chemical warfare."

"It's fairly obvious what this world has done to both of us, Stark. It's taken everything and left us with nothing---except each other."

"Under different circumstances, that would be more than enough. But right now, we need a way out. Oh God, it's no use, JeZe Bella. This city is a maze. I'm running around in circles. If I could only get my mind right! "The words were getting lost between his brain and his tongue; he knew he was talking nonsense. The odds were all against them and after a time, Barry realized that he had no idea where he was. Trapped in New York City that he had known all his life, he tried to read the name of the streets but the letters danced around themselves.

The moments were passing by in slow motion. "The thought of drifting by traffic lights only makes me feel lonely." Barry mused. "Oh now, don't cry. JeZe Bella. We'll make it somehow as long as we are together."

Ominously, on Times Square, a black and white police cruiser moved up discreetly, inching its way alongside them as they paused for a red light. Barry turned and gave the officer a cynical salute, noticing then that the cruiser contained two young recruits who did not look familiar.

"Roger, car 54 to headquarters," one of the rookie officers reported with an air of authority, "I have matched description of male and female to all-Points Bulletin. Have Corvette, Long Island plate 4SLUG in sight. Please advise, 10-4."

"Roger!" came the shriek reply. "Proceed with extreme caution. Suspects believed armed and dangerous. All units will be dispatched shortly for assistance and back-up, 10-4."

In a venturesome way, the patrol car kept them in sight for a considerable distance. High above, under vigilant eyes of the night a police helicopter hovered above, tracking the vehicle on its radar screen. Up ahead, a police roadblock had been formed, as sirens screamed from behind and the police car's strobe red, white and blue lights penetrated the tense air like a relentless beacon.

"Lord, no stop sticks!" Barry accelerated the car, please to see that the engine was instantly responsive and generous with its horsepower. Disregarding a slight detour to the right of the street, he glanced at JeZe Bella and asked, "Are you with me all the way, babe?"

"Yes, Stark---all the way," JeZe Bella assured him calmly. As the words seemed to die on her lips, the Corvette lurched forward to his heavy-footed command. In a vexing, teasing manner, the car slid around corners and streaked down the avenue, now dangerously out of control as Barry's sense of panic increased.

As the two police officers gave chase, they both knew that this day's action would be forever engraved on their minds. As they watched, the gleaming sports car rolled erratically and then plunge on a vertical path, coming to rest upon the wide Catholic Church steps.

"Well, even if he were Satan himself, he's done for now," one of the witnessing officers observed prophetically as they came to a squealing stop.

Soon, part of the decadent crowd on the street gathered round, while the alarming sound of the crash drew parishioners from inside the church. On this Good Friday, a late mass had been underway; even as the roaring sounds of sirens gripped the air profusely no one else was hurt outside on the steps.

In the final moments, death hung waiting a fiery coffin. There was no further determination left in Barry's bleeding body.

He had skirted death once too often, after winning so many times before. Now ravaged and exhausted, he hung strapped upside down in the car, too physically weak to work himself free in order to save himself and Jeze Bella.

Fatally injured, JeZe Balla looked straight into his green eyes, her brown eyes compelling him to recognize her at that special moment. Her faded red lips were parted slightly, and he could almost hear her "I'm with say, all the you I'll follow way, you Barry to hell if that is what I have to do to be with you forever."

In that most sensationally satisfying moment, the terror of death was replaced by the promise of relief from both physical and his mental pain. As they lay pinned upside down in the over turned car, in a watery pool of gasoline, a flicker of some momentary joy illuminated their faces, even as a small tear rolled from the corner of Barry's eye. Then, as his lighted cigarette fell from his mouth, igniting a fiery blast, as tall glass buildings near by shuddered profusely in the aftershock the sounds of breaking window glass shattered the air around.

The yellow tape was rolled out as the police shielded and supervised the secured area; a fire truck arrived to douse the flames with special foam.

Working his way through the sadistic horror of the moment, Chief Abraham assumed control and flinched slightly as his nostrils caught a whiff of the acrid smoke. He could see all too clearly what was left of Barry Stark's partially charred remains and the body of the young woman beside him. Held their moment in time like a lover's embrace as his police badge had flipped out the car window in the blast and laid now on the church steps.

It was an unimaginable event for the jittery horde of shouting reporters and the video camera news crews. Those who stood amid the clouds of choking smoke and debris were thought to be thick-skinned because of their affiliation. With the news media, but they swept back in an uncertain manner when Chief Abraham arrived at the scene. After a brief moment, someone said, "Is that him. He's dead?" making the question sounds more like a statement and not a fact.

"In what was a most friendly of fire?" Another well-intention young newsman said, looking for a new twist on the breaking story of the year.

"Everything is a little tense, huh boys?" Abraham suggested with a wan smile. "Well, it'll probably stay that way for the next few days."

A young reporter, countered in a defiant manner, "You sound like have mixed reaction about this renegade cop." you

"Well, son he was a most reluctant subject, and was dying of impatience and some misguided rebellion against society, in which morals didn't much matter anymore." This information was grudgingly admitted. "Yet, it was sadly inappropriate that the circumstances did not allow him to die in peace. It sounds ludicrous now, but his exaggeration of reality was stopped cold-right here, tonight." He heard a muffled grumbling, followed by the voice of yet another reporter.

"But, chief---he must have had a very complex motive."

"Hell, a psychiatrist would argue that, I suppose. Unfortunately, such a desirable outcome rarely occurs in the life of a man such as Barry Stark. No sooner does the serious underlying disturbance surface, and there is failure, frustration and further unhappiness. He soon falls into a fantasy like the young beautiful model whose life died beside him tonight." The Chief paused to wipe the beads of moisture from his brow.

At that point, as if coming to his rescue, Lieutenant Bloodworth stepped in. halting beside the Chief, he spoke quickly and under his breath. "Look, these reporters are asking too many questions." Even as he spoke, the media crowded in, trying to catch the rift of their conversation over Stark's reign of terror.

"If I may respectfully suggest something to you, Chief, I'd like to say that I think it would be best to drop this PTSD thing for now. Stark is dead and the proof has all but gone up in smoke. If you don't abandon the subject right now, you'll have to see it through to the bitter end." It was a well-intention warning in the very midst of the hard press cover around them.

"Make no mistake, Lieutenant," Abraham quickly retaliated, "I've listened to your quick tongue before."

Bloodworth threw the Chief a bitter glance, and then leaned forward, holding the reporters motionless with his gaze.

"Lieutenant, what is all this about PTSD and Barry Stark?" a veteran female reporter injected pointedly as if she had a secret source of medical information.

"Hog wash! These particular police officer had serious mental problems. A psychotic's rights are determined by an extremely fine line. There are those among us, even now, whose concept of reality is so twisted and distorted, that it is no more responsible than Barry Stark's view of life. Let me stress again that Stark was a 918-that's police jargon for an insane person."

"But Lieutenant!" the female reporter persisted. "Are you aware of certain accusations that were made earlier today by Professor Oliver Reed?"

"This is outrageous!" Bloodworth expounded. "Oliver Reed has nothing to do with this case. Perhaps you're not aware of that, my dear. Suffice to say that Reed's conjectures amount to little more than a politician's tricks. I think your media people should find out what office he's running for next."

"Mellow out, Lieutenant," another reporter suggested snidely. "You sound as if you wouldn't lift a finger to help your own mother."

"Leave my mother out of this, "Bloodworth snapped impatiently.

"The subject at hand concerns itself with the tricky tactics of a professor who seems to be on some self-serving mission. Whatever he's got in mind, I'm sure he'll profit from it. Concerning this PTSD matter, you might ask yourselves if he is really the complainant in the case or if he is only using the event. There seems to be a queer notion of honesty here. It's one of those things where one can actually cheat a dead man who was, after all, an unhappy victim of the tragedy. As for me, well ...I couldn't do that. The victim might be anyone's brother or son-if you know what I mean."

"Who could criticize you, Lieutenant Bloodworth? Your philosophy taints the whole ugly picture."

The lieutenant thought he detected a hint of mockery in the reporter's level gaze. "Face it," he said bluntly. "I'll take advantage of every opportunity you people hand me, just to show a few people how foolish they really are." He looked long and hard, but found no revelation among them.

When, Chief Abraham pushed forward with a display of cheerfulness he did not really feel. "What's left to say?" he asked in a reasonable tone. "This Oliver Reed is dead wrong." He gave a curt nod, trying to remain patient. "All I can ask of your newspaper people is that a wrong be righted,"

It was startling the way the impulsive news media flocked over the strained situation. There was a most uncomfortable feeling present-like defeat-as several of the police sank back in a group. But there was no simple way to evaluate the moment of friends or foe in the climate of police distrust.

"All one can surmise is that he must have had an emotionally disturbed childhood-without love or caring," one wide-eyed warm leatherneck cop stated.

"Strange, isn't it?" another reflected without a trace of irony in his voice. "This poor devil did something we only dream of doing, but that's only because our job is to preserve the law, not destroy it."

Across the street was the worst technical nightmare imaginable the live video camera trucks had rolled on location with co-anchor woman, Ana Happy Shaw doing her nightly on-the-spot interviews.

"Sergeant Romero, you worked with him once. Why don't you tell the Action News viewers a bit about Barry Stark?" she initiated after a brief silence.

"I met him five-and-a-half years ago. He was a capable cop then, with an easy-going style that was both disarming and canny. Once upon a time, he was a bright, personable fellow." The sergeant hooked his thumbs into his gun belt as a film of moisture momentarily veiled his brown eyes. "It is impossible to imagine a more faithful or brilliant end to this case."

"Sergeant, would you feel it's fair to say that he was a cop who administered his own brand of justice?'

"Yes, because he seemed very disappointed in the performance of our justice system. In that respect, who could blame him? Still, it's kind of sad. Maybe the people of New York City will forget him in time." After a long, thoughtful moment, he added, "What I've said shouldn't be misconstrued as evidence-these are just my own feelings."

"Thank you, Sergeant Romero, for being most candid and honest," Shaw said with a smile. "Well viewers, you heard the solemn sergeant say that it was hard to comprehend any of this, and even harder to accept that these tragic events ever happened. And for you people just tuning in, this is Ana Happy Shaw, reporting live from St. Mathew's Catholic Cathedral square where Officer Barry Stark died only moments ago. The fatal accident occurred about 9:30 p.m. as the stolen car in which he and his female companion were riding, slid around the corner and literally plowed into the church steps at 60 m.p.h. Soon afterwards, the car burst into flames." She seemed intensely concerned as she leaned toward the camera. "Well folks, I have here stood beside me, our own city's mayor, Pete

McCain. Mayor, I wonder if you would be kind enough to share your feelings with us now that this brutal case has been solved."

"What is irksome about this case," McCain replied, "is that the case is not yet truly solved. I'm convinced that Barry Stark did not work alone- that, in fact, others on the police force cooperated, aiding and abetting him in this succession of murders." His message fell on everyone's ears like a blanket indictment.

"That's certainly a strong statement," Shaw acknowledged sternly, sensing his personal hatred for the police department, and more particularly, for Chief Abraham.

"I am here to assure the people of New York City that this case will not be white-washed, and will remain open for a few months, while a number of private investigators pursue the matter further." Basking in the limelight, he paused significantly before adding, "It is my own opinion that we will successfully accumulate the needed evidence. I also believe that someone will inevitably step forward."

"So then, Mayor, you are publicly alleging at this time that Barry Stark was involved in a conspiracy?"

The mayor returned her intimidating gaze and felt him stiffening against the challenge. He did not answer her immediately. He seemed embarrassed now, uncomfortable. Shaw sensed that there was something amiss as she turned away from him like a playful seal. He hadn't the time to size up his adversary as he strained to hear what she was saying in the close-up to her cameras.

"From our nightly on-the-spot news, this is Ana Happy Shaw saying, 'Here is New York-the town, its people, its art, its neon. Ever destined, to be the culture capitol of the world, even while it is veiled in mystery, murder, and even ready to emerge in splendor in the hustle and bustle of everyday life. Goodnight, all."

The city soon shrouded itself in mist as a smell of polluted river water crept in, clinging to everything in the damp of the night.

This set the action during this night's motorcycle patrol on its citizens. To capture the squalor of humanity that hid beneath and among the grimy exterior of what was New York City. With its thugs, boozy twists, porn and meth head's that attracted the attention of the police force like a loud buzz on their beats. As they passed the creeps under the street corner lights.

Who smoked weed on the curb and worked on their brown bagged malt liquor bottles? While mad red-faced as hell cops were not surprised as their testosterone built up inside them. Amid those Latino's and African Americans who followed up with horded name-calling to draw the cops into a police brutality scene. For hell has no fury would be its theme in the city's surreal reality.

CLOSED-CASKET

CHAPTER 29

IN THE GOLDEN brightness of the afternoon, on the Monday after Easter Sunday, a crowd had gathered outside the chapel doors to listen to the closed-casket service for Officer Barry Stark. New York police officers placed purple shrouds across the badges over their hearts and saluted bravely as the body of their comrade was placed in the waiting white hearse. From there it was escorted to the Holy Cross Memorial Park Cemetery while noon-hour traffic came to an abrupt halt along the busy avenues.

Motorists gawked at some 500 helmeted motorcycle policemen who led the solemn procession across town. Unexpectedly, a bus driver slid opens his window and saluted. A young lady in the next lane sat inside her car, wiping away the tears of sorrow and joy for some.

"This funeral is about as low profile as it can get with all the opinionated news press standing around us," Chief Abraham observed sagely. "And none of them can say that we don't take care of our own men in blue, regardless."

"True Chief but it's not over for us. The rumor has it we have another choir-boy on the loose, who serves his own brand of justice. With three new murders since Stark's horrific death." Lieutenant Bloodworth speculated.

"No, I guess we did not break the mold when we last hired Barry Stark, now I have another rogue cop on my hands. When will all this end?" the chief replied sadly and stooped his head as he heard the eulogy start on this bad note.

"Dear Lord, there are a lot of things we may never understand about Barry Stark," reverend Donald McDougall invoked in a tone that was solemnly respectful. "But he was a husband and father, and is survived by two small sons. O' God, whose most dear Son has taken Barry Stark, give us grace, we beseech thee, to entrust the soul of this man to thy never-failing care and love as we commit his body to the ground. May the Lord bless him and keep him, Amen." The reverend stood up from his knees and closed his Bible as a sign that the service was concluded. Then he looked across the plain black coffin that was draped with a *warm leather* jacket as a thousand mourners stood outside the cemetery gates realizing that blue lives matter, whatever the circumstances.

Amid the solemnity of the occasion, two policemen worked their way slowly through the crowd with bowed heads and slumped shoulders. Thoughtfully one asked the other in a voice barely above a whisper, "I wonder if it's true...I mean about Barry Stark's PTSD?"

"Well finally congress has started to move, to get these Vets the help they deserve for God's sake and it took our Barry Stark, to wake them up as the DOJ has announced a study and research on PTSD and our president is 100 % behind it."

PRELUDE TO WARM LEATHER
CHAPTER 30

In the wee hours with an instinct for the taste of blood this motorcycle cop stood tall and cold as stone in the gloom of nightfall. Confident and instinctively his eyes needed time to adjust to the blackened of the darkness around him. While his glaring stare focus on the surroundings. He had followed a bad guy into a well-known crony bar that had a small dance floor as he walked pass underneath a twirling disco crystal ball, he noticed his next victim at the dark end of the bar. With some satisfaction, was there deception hidden beneath his gaze - his bashful-brown-orbs were set deep into his facial features. Having a lite-cough the man in the corner looked up at him. The officer than reached down under his belt and shafted a knife sideways into the man's sternum. Who dropped without a sound or breath to the dirty floor? The cop suddenly felt the cold handle of his gun brush up against his manly palm - instantly there was an icy chill of air at his neck. With a quick and most fluid motion he spun around in his black boots and walked out into the neon night from which he had come.

"Holly shit, there is a man on the floor!" a patron yelled: as this peace-loving officer rode off with the wind beating down against his *warm leather* jacket on a gleaming black and white Harley Davidson motorcycle. In what was a good night for a kill? He knew more about the nature of this terrible evil that seek to impose itself on the streets of New York City and the Lady of Justice. This cop will never fear his own shadow as the newest most wanted man who was at the very top of Chief Abraham's list. The high-stakes for him could not be greater in the fast-pace world of the city, filled with action, crime, betrayal, sex, adultery, money, romance and cold-blooded murder. In this intense political charge society. This is a cop who now answers the bell as he mows down the stooges and throws them to the ground and makes them kiss his shiny black boots. In his neon universe there was no questions asked with a contract on him as an assassin in this big city. His new violence is relentless and a mayhem as he is the second cop to follow Barry Stark's footsteps. On exactly the same path and passion for justice on behalf of Barry who never flinch. Still, he is cool and he would do whatever a man must do- in his *warm leather* jacket that had a nice sensibility to it. His was no urban fantasy at the end of a dark alley. Where there are something's to fear like a lavish drug party that turned deadly and having a hard time identifying the most likely of suspects. With certain surly swagger, this new cop on the block, a mean bastard through and through, nameless for now as he lurks behind in the shadows. New York City was now about to find out that the one thing more dangerous than Barry Stark is another mortal-cop. Who may have been his closest ally behind the gold badge? Yes, he too is thought of as another black sheep on the Metro Police force. But not as a sacrificial lamb, this officer of the law had to be regarded with suspicion and disdain like Barry Stark, as he too was eager to leap into action while on his job. Knowing a single mistake could cost him, his head. No matter as he carried a burning grudge against those who bended the rule of law. Because when you live by the sword, you must be prepared to die on the sword. While the setting sun broiled the city's black asphalt streets the agony of the night heat begins as hell's firkin fire blurted out his conscious and manly form, mocking and full of spite. He spat the ground beneath his feet that exploded with a pounding wind out of his chest that reverberated in the filth around him........ for this officer was Roman Vargas, a tall young well-built Puerto Rican. This man would never purposely sidestep an order before some judge that was considered justified in his mind. On any night of nights, he turns on to the streets and looks into the distance over his shoulder. To cuss as he feels his minty tooth-paste breath brush up his face -- showing no mercy like the sweet kiss of death from an avenging angel.

Leaving no doubt behind except the loud blaring raucous sound of his motorcycle to echo and vibrate in the cool breeze against his *Warm Leather* jacket.... as he joins up with his partner. A black officer, Fredrick Blake for some hot coffee and doughnuts. As he speeded pass some bible thumpers standing on a corner preaching, 'End times and end of days.' The prefect ending to his long night and a fresh kill that still burned in his nostrils.

www.ingramcontent.com/pod-product-compliance
Lightning Source LLC
LaVergne TN
LVHW021819060526
838201LV00058B/3444